Love's Body, Dancing in the critically acclaimed L. T could tell. Carnal and queer, from the heart-breaking St the Edge" and the historically authentic, Tiptree snort-listed  "The Apprenticeship of Isabetta di Pietro Cavazzi," to the subtle, original "The Héloïse Archive," in which the rewriting of the eleventh-century abbess's life story dramatically alters the course of European history. Like all of Duchamp's work, this fiction is passionate, feminist, and intelligent.

Advance Praise for *Love's Body, Dancing in Time*:

"This handful of SF tales demonstrates superbly what the genre can really do. Rich with social resonance, these stories elicit the thrill of ideas struggling to manifest as pure drama. Duchamp writes some of the most rewarding science fiction stories you can read today; she is simply and unarguably among the best."

—Samuel R. Delany, author of *Dhalgren* and *Nova*.

"These stories create a delicate choreography of longing, love and loss. They continue to perform in the mind long after you've turned the last page."

—Nalo Hopkinson, author of *The Salt Roads* and *Brown Girl in the Ring*.

Tiptree Juror comments on "The Apprenticeship of Isabetta di Pietro Cavazzi":

"One of the great pleasures this novelette presented as excerpts from a diary is the effortless way in which Duchamp recreates the Italy of 1629. This historicity helps put over the story of a young woman coming to understand her supernatural powers in the wake of an unhappy love affair. Duchamp convinces me that if witches existed, this is what they'd be like."

—James P. Kelly, author of *Strange But Not a Stranger*

Love's Body, Dancing in Time

L. Timmel Duchamp

Aqueduct Press

Published by Aqueduct Press
PO Box 95787
Seattle, WA 98145-2787
www.aqueductpress.com

Copyright © 2004 L. Timmel Duchamp

Library of Congress Control Number: 2003098096
Library of Congress Cataloging in Publication Data
Duchamp, L. Timmel, 1950-
Love's Body, Dancing in Time
L. Timmel Duchamp, 1st ed.
1. key term—Abelard and Héloïse, fiction. 2. key term—
gender politics, fiction. 3. science fiction. 4. fantastic
fiction.
ISBN 0-9746559-1-0
First Edition, First Printing, April 2004

"The Apprenticeship of Isabetta di Pietro Cavazzi"
originally appeared in *Asimov's SF*, September, 1997, (c) L.
Timmel Duchamp, 1997

"Dance at the Edge" originally appeared in Nicola Griffith
& Stephen Pagel, eds., *Bending the Landscape: Science
Fiction*, Overlook Press, September, 1998 (c) L. Timmel
Duchamp, 1998

Cover Photographs by Thomas Duchamp: front, Rievaulx
Abbey, Yorkshire, England, August 1978; back, Boboli
Gardens in Firenze, Italy, July 1978.

Cover Design by Lynne Jensen Lampe
Printed in the USA

Contents

A society, then, is not a fixed and stable entity but an always shifting, always changing process. In fact, a considerable amount of cultural work is required to maintain the illusion of stasis and permanence, to deny the workings of complexity in and through society. In a more complex, "disorderly" model, societies both maintain themselves and change through elaborate feedback mechanisms by which their cultural productions— individuals, genders, class identities, and written texts— feedback into them, reorganizing and reproducing social structures and the strategies that maintain and refashion them.

—Laurie A. Finke *Feminist Theory, Women's Writing*

Indeed, the present always seems to be in the way. Between us and the past, in which lie events we might wish to recover or redo, as between us and the future, in which our desires might be satisfied, our ambitions fulfilled, or our visions realized, the present, though vexatiously elusive and seemingly momentary and minute, remains inescapably in place . . . . What we call the present is, to use Nietzsche's phrase, "the duration of 'the impermanence of everything actual'." "The present" is the name for the span during which the transitoriness, the finitude, of everything we identify as "real" exists.

—Lyn Hejinian, "A Common Sense"

Dance at the Edge

1.

Emma Persimmon discovered the Edge in the first month of her life. Chance gave her a glimpse of starscape, of a black denser than that of simple night, of a glittering spray of lights as splendid and desirable as a gold pendant dangling just out of reach. How it fascinated her infant self! It was the very second thing she pointed at; and countless times a day it made her giggle and stretch her fingers to grasp.

At five months, Emma knew where to look to see the Edge and that it was different from everything else and always changing. Suddenly able to crawl, she raced to enter it— only to discover that touching made it recede (or sometimes even vanish altogether). The large, strange, shaggy creatures splashing about in a mud hole were there, yes, to her eyes, but not to her hands, fingers, toes, mouth. Emma learned she could crawl to the Edge and occupy the space where something else had been, and the Edge would leap back, and instead of a mud hole, there would be just the floor, just the air, just herself. . . In this, Emma resembled most babies. They, like her, played *fort/da* with the Edge. But at least one of Emma's parents did not pretend to her infant self that the Edge did not exist, although as Emma grew older, that parent of course denied ever seeing it.

By the time she started attending school, Emma understood that any acknowledgment of its presence was beyond "bad," "naughty," and "unacceptable." Even so, Emma got in trouble her very first day. The Edge in her classroom lay along the back wall, out of her proper line of vision. Usually in such new circumstances the Edge would have been easy to resist. But the Edge in her classroom that day was not just any Edge. It was a scene of a desert wash so full of light that whenever Emma looked at it straight on, she reflexively put her hand up to shield her eyes from a glare that she only, of course, imagined. Through the rocky wash trickled a thin silver stream of water, in which grew long thick grasses, tiny jewel-like blossoms of sapphire, topaz, and garnet, and tall willows, lush with mauve trumpet-shaped flowers and long slim leaves. Tiny green birds with fantastically long beaks hovered over the willows, wings whirring, dipping their needle-like beaks into the bells of the flowers they courted and drained in exuberant, darting dance. Emma's parents had taught her about bees and nectar and pollen. It excited her almost unbearably to think that these strange little birds were probably doing what bees did. The classroom, by comparison, seemed dull and stupid.

Emma, young model of propriety, did not openly stare over her shoulder; rather she stole glances from the side. But— "Emma Persimmon!" The teacher's voice cracked like a whip, making Emma jump guiltily. "What are you doing, staring off into space, daydreaming?" The tone of the teacher's voice clearly implied that *daydreaming* was among the worst crimes a student could commit. Emma almost cried with humiliation. Obediently she stared straight ahead, directly at the teacher, for several minutes. But unused to sitting in a classroom, increasingly fidgeting and restless, she forgot— and turned her head to snatch just a glimpse. "Look at Emma Persimmon," the teacher said almost at once. Jeering: "Off in her own little world."

The children copied the teacher's words every chance they got, tormenting Emma with the confidence of the unthinking young.

No, Emma wanted to protest. *Not off in my own world, off in* another *world.* But just a kindergartner, she lacked the words for talking about the socially invisible and knew the whole present world against her. So she kept quiet and grew very shy and strove mightily never again to be seen staring at that wall in the classroom (though she still stared often enough to get a reputation for daydreaming).

Most children let go of the Edge in their earliest years. Emma Persimmon never did. Instead, she wondered how the teacher, facing it, could so easily pretend not to see it and, later, whether others even saw it at all. And since everyone— even the one parent who acknowledged its reality during Emma's preschool years— acted so completely as if they did not see it, she finally understood that at least in one sense they did not. By the time she was sixteen, Emma began to wonder if it was even really there and not just something she'd been fantasizing all her life.

The need to avoid social opprobrium can be truly terrible, not to say terrifying and terrorizing. Emma carried it all inside, afraid to whisper a word of it to anyone— until her parents sent her to town for training in the Ecohusbandry Guild, and she met Viola Knight.

2.

The moment Emma Persimmon laid eyes on her, she thought Viola Knight the bee's knees. Clad in tailored muslin pajamas, she stood straight and smart, brushing her teeth with a style that literally took Emma's breath away. Oh such beauty, Emma thought inanely, transfixed by the graceful precision of a wrist bone framed by elegant pajama cuff. Emma, stationed at another basin, fiddled with her bath kit, eyes glued to that wrist in the mirror, and forgot to brush her own teeth.

Viola Knight, thorough in all she did, never noticed.

Emma returned to her room, burning with that all-consuming awareness. She fought off sleep for most of the night, tormented by images of the lovely wrist and perfect white sleeve, until sunrise tricked her into a doze.

Viola Knight, lost in the fascination of the Elementary Principles of Optics, never much noticed anybody who didn't shove themselves right up into her face. Emma, though, now living for even the most fleeting glimpse of the divine object of her desire, almost forgot the Edge existed. When her genetics instructor caught her mooning, it wasn't for staring at the Edge, but for doodling hand after hand of thick, strong, spatulate fingers and comely, sharp-boned wrist, compulsively, religiously, intemperately.

Emma had it bad.

3.

In her first three months in town— before she saw Viola Knight brushing her teeth— Emma had taken to hanging out with a disparate collection of individuals living in her dorm, all apprentices in arts guilds. They amused her and easily swept her into their intense personal dramas and fantasies. With them she developed the beginnings of confidence in her capacity for existing socially. For the first time in her life she discovered a tolerance for the "daydreaming" and eccentricity people of her own sort found by turns irritating and disquieting.

She attended a play with them her second week in town. It struck her that the very idea of a staged drama must have come from *somebody's* awareness of the Edge, and this insight plunged her afresh into her old metaphysical questions. Were all of these creative people attracted to the arts because they sensed— but had been taught to ignore— that it was there? Or did they all know it was there and seek somehow to replicate it in such a way that their audiences would see it without a loss of innocence as to the real Edge they did not? As bright and imaginative as she found her new friends, Emma did not dare speak any of her questions aloud.

Quickly Emma slid into a sort of niche with them. She made them laugh, but with pleasure at— rather than to mock— her rather ingenuous wonder. She did not know why they accepted her, only that they did. But she discovered her position among them to be conspicuous when at dinner, a few nights after Emma's body began burning for Viola, Letitia Shadows murmured, "For shame, Emma Persimmon," as Emma's eyes tracked Viola Knight all the way from the salad bar back to a table of engineering apprentices. "Inspired by the slide-rule over the cello."

"Both instruments celebrate the abstract," Paulus Square, the only cellist present, said. Pale and unsmiling, he bowed across the table at them, his austere body virtually as abstract as either calculus or music.

"People have been known to fall in love with paintings, statues, and vases," Royal Quiet said.

"But I'll take someone with a warm, juicy body, any day," Elizabeth Peartree said.

"Yes," Letitia Shadows said, sounding sad. "Someone like Emma Persimmon, whose body, in the perception of my senses, bursts with heat and juices like a peach hanging ripe in the sun."

Emma blushed hotly and denied nothing. She glanced sidelong to the far reaches of the room where Viola Knight sat, only a meter or so from the Edge.

"Never fear," Paulus Square said to Emma. "She'll never know— unless you tell her yourself."

Emma sighed, relieved and disappointed when she believed him, relieved and fearful when she did not. She was amazed that they had seen her passion without her speaking it. Why, then, would Viola Knight herself not see it, too?

4.

Surely it was inevitable that Emma Persimmon's ardent devotion to Viola Knight would eventually bear fruit. Had not all the famous Fated Lovers of their world, from its earliest history, always come— eventually— together, even those from distant villages or feuding guilds? Emma hoped, feared, believed that her own desire combined with simple proximity must make it happen.

One Saturday afternoon, Emma followed Viola Knight onto a bus to the edge of town and from there on foot into the forest. She stalked and tracked Viola Knight with no subtlety whatsoever, flying from one inadequately-shielding tree-trunk to another, frequently catching her flowing red scarf on the bare winter thorns, wincing often at the racket her sneakered tippy-toes made as they scuffled gold, red, and brown leaves and fractured sharp, dry twigs. When Viola Knight came to a stream, followed its banks for a few yards, and then trod a narrow log to cross it, Emma's desire grew giddy. Flitting and gliding after Viola, ever deeper into gloomy, fern-loving wood, Emma knew the delirious thrill of the hunt and the delicious chill of the possibility that the hunter, discovered, might herself become the hunted.

Then Viola Knight stood stock-still, hands on hips, head thrust slightly forward in total, utter concentration. Emma took a look around— and gasped. Viola had brought her to an Edge. A huge, stunning, exceptionally wonderful Edge. *Out of doors.*

Viola Knight walked along its face— and then turned sharply, where the Edge actually seemed to come to a point, as though it were an acute angle— and walked along an apparent *second* face. Emma, so astonished that she forgot her purpose in tracking Viola, unthinkingly followed and saw for herself that *this* Edge was actually wedge-shaped, like a sliver of giant pie plopped down right there in the middle of the forest.

And what a pie it was! Emma Persimmon had always been more enchanted by the existence of the Edge than by the things she usually saw beyond it. But beyond— or rather *inside*— this three-dimensional wedge of an Edge glittered a world unlike any she had ever seen. Wild gouts of flame poured out of torches topping twisted cast-iron rods that had been placed among bizarrely-shaped trees, brilliantly illuminating the immediate areas around them, creating dark, impenetrable pockets of shadow. Willowy human figures wove in and out of the torches and trees, their faces painted the cloud-white of their stockinged legs, their eyes, mouths, and eyebrows heavily outlined in thick black paint. All of them wore scarlet, gold, and purple knee-length coats over tight black bodices and black silver-buckled, blockily highheeled boots they stamped smartly each time their hands came together in a clapping Emma Persimmon fancied she could almost *hear*. They spun. They jumped. They clapped and stamped. They leaped. The intricacy of their dance surpassed any Emma had ever known.

Emma forgot Viola Knight altogether. So fiercely did she concentrate on extrapolating the rhythm from the dance that she heard nothing but it. And peering into a scene of night, she forgot that though dim, the forest in which *she* stood lay in full— albeit cloudy— daylight.

Viola Knight turned and paced back toward the vertex of the Edge. And since she, too, never took her eyes off the entrancing scene, she ran smack into Emma.

Yanked out of their common dream, they stared at one another in shock. Viola's eyes blazed; she grabbed Emma's arm. "You're the girl who's always following me into the bathroom!"

Emma Persimmon's heart beat violently hard; her breath caught in her throat. The moment seemed lifted out of a traditional romance, for Viola's grip on her arm was steely enough to leave a substantial bruise afterwards. She realized that Viola had, indeed, noticed her existence. "Yes," Emma said breathily. "I live across the hall from you. Emma Persimmon."

"Emma Persimmon," Viola Knight repeated with near-disbelief. "What kind of name is that?"

Emma's body oozed and throbbed with sexual excitement. Their dialogue was going exactly the way it should! What more could a girl in love ask for?

A quicksilver flash of color— torchlight catching the sequins powdering the fat white towers of curls topping the dancers' heads as they all bowed in unison— distracted Emma, reminding her of what she had momentarily forgotten. Her heart lifted in wildest exultation. "You see it, you actually see it!"

Viola Knight looked puzzled. "See what?"

Emma's heart sank. She jerked her head at the dancers. "You aren't going to claim you don't see the Edge, are you? You've been walking alongside it and staring in on all those strange people dancing. I know you have, I saw you do it!" Emma swallowed; heat scoured her face. Since coming to town she had not been mocked even once for her sin of Edge-watching. The very thought that Viola Knight, of all people, might now be mocking her was devastating.

Viola Knight's eyebrows shot high in her elegant broad forehead. "The Seam, you mean? You called it what— an edge?"

"Seam!" Emma said, shivering with more excitement than she could hold quietly inside her.

Viola looked at her curiously. "Oh," she said. "Did you run a little too forcefully into the denial all the people in town profess?" She shook her head. "Really, it's so childish. I must say I'll be happy when I've finished my studies and can return to my village, where no one plays such silly, jejune games."

Emma Persimmon was stunned. "Your village— you're saying that all the people there see the Edge, too?"

"You mean the people in your own village act like those in town?" Viola shook her head. "But that figures, I suppose. Apparently all the guilds but mine follow the same silly line on Seams."

Emma's eyes shone more brightly than any of the torches lighting the world beyond the Edge. She wanted to dance for joy, or, rather, drop to her knees and kiss the toe of her adored one's soft leather boot, the only gesture she could imagine capable of giving full expression to the power of her feelings. She touched Viola's arm timidly (not daring, of course, even to approach her wrist). "So the people in your village and guild call them Seams? Do you know what they are, and where they come from? Or why most people don't seem to see them at all?"

5.

Viola Knight and Emma Persimmon walked out of the forest side by side. They walked as separate individuals, without touching, but listening to Viola expound on "Seams," Emma took pleasure simply in hearing the sound of Viola's voice and feeling the heat of Viola's body.

"Oh," Viola Knight said. She frowned sidelong at Emma. "I've just realized. My parents warned me that a prerequisite of certification is taking an oath to preserve the guild's secrets, which include everything we know or have theorized about Seams, even their very existence."

Emma halted to face Viola. "Which would mean that after certification you couldn't, for instance, let me know that you saw what I was seeing back there in the forest?" Her excitement in finding another person in the world who saw the Edge, her pleasure in finally sharing company with this most wonderful of persons, drained out of Emma. Her body went stone, dread cold. The implications of Viola's words struck her like a blow to the solar plexus. She saw it all too clearly: that everything— the very world she lived in— was false— and wrong, terribly, terribly wrong.

Viola Knight put her hand to her throat, under the thick black scarf protecting it. "Oh shit," she said. "What a fuck-up." Her eyes searched Emma's face. "I could be thrown out of the program for having this conversation with you. I'm not under an oath yet, no, but if the masters ever found out, I'd never make it to certification." She blinked. "We have all these rules for apprentices, you know. Like not using a hand-held calculator for the first two years, to make sure that we all get to be proficient in using slide-rules. But because I hardly know anyone who isn't an engineer, I never much thought about the Silence-About-Seams rule."

Emma felt guilty for putting Viola's future in jeopardy— and then crazy, too, for feeling guilty. Her heart pounded in the thick, nauseating silence that made her feel as though she were smothering. "Don't you realize how *terrible* your guild's silence is? It's nearly ruined my life— making me worry all the time that I might be crazy. I'm sure there are people who *do* go crazy, never knowing what's real and what's not!"

Viola's lips parted. "Oh," she said softly. "They told me people were trained to block Seams out of their vision, like the floaters in one's eyes. They said that only engineers ever saw them at all." Her eyes darkened in sweet, dewy softness. "I'm sorry, Emma, I'm so very, very sorry. But at least now you do know."

They resumed walking, and Viola revealed some of what she knew about what the Seams were and what little she had been told about why people were taught not to see them. Since Emma had no idea even what a particle was, Viola's mini-lecture on tachyon fields meant nothing to her. But when Viola told her about how in earlier times people had made religions and claimed powers of divination from the appearances of particular Seams, Emma listened with rapt attention.

"They were, in effect, used to manipulate large groups of people," Viola said as they came within sight of the bus, parked at the terminus. "There were terrible wars as a result. And so it was decided that it would be best if people just pretended they weren't there. Seeing how easily certain persons could use them to manipulate large groups of people. And so everyone did forget them— except the engineers, who swore themselves to secrecy. Well, it stood to reason, you know. It's not as though we *could* ignore them. And so they became a sort of trade secret." Viola fell silent at the sight of the driver leaning against the bus, reading. They greeted her and asked her how long before the bus returned to town.

The driver consulted the digital readout on the cuff of her sleeve. "Three minutes, twenty seconds," she said.

Viola Knight and Emma Persimmon boarded the bus. Since they could not talk about the forbidden subject in the presence of a non-engineer, Viola asked Emma about her village and guild. Only later did Emma realize that Viola had not asked her why she had followed her out of town, into the woods, in the first place.

6.

In the days following, both the pleasure of Emma's love and the pain of its being unspoken and unreturned intensified. Emma grew self-conscious in her surveillance of Viola. Instead of being emboldened by the advance in their relationship, Emma grew fearful of causing offense. Her friends, having seen that the two were now acquainted, teased Emma, trying to prod her into open pursuit. "Seduce her," Letitia Shadows said. "She won't be able to resist! Not *you*, Emma."

Emma began, for the first time, to spend long hours in the library so that she could "brood in peace," as she thought of it. She assumed that sitting in the Biology section would preserve her from her friends' scrutiny. But she had not counted on the need of art students to consult biology texts in their search for tropes.

"Emma Persimmon, what on earth is all that?"

Emma was doodling— the usual, of course. She looked up guiltily at Sanctus Geloso, then back down at her screen. She made a jab for the Clear button, but Sanctus caught her wrist and stopped her. "Sanctus," she whispered in protest, but the name came out little more than a hiss.

Sanctus Geloso's scowl was fierce. "Why representational drawing?" he asked, though not whispering, keeping his voice low. "Why not thieve a piece of her clothing, or hair, or the damned toothbrush?"

Emma realized that she was getting good at drawing not only Viola Knight's wrist and pajama sleeve, but her hand holding the toothbrush as well. So good, she thought, looking now at the doodling she usually erased after she'd finished a screenful, that she actually felt like tracing her finger over the screen as a substitute for touching the real thing.

"I love those hands," Emma Persimmon said. "I just love them. If I could sculpt the way you do, I'd make a pair of them in marble, and it would be *wonderful*."

Sanctus Geloso was shocked. He insisted that Emma go with him for coffee, so that they could talk. That's what he *said*. But once he got Emma outside the library, out into the cold, frosty air, he began lecturing her like a parent who has discovered his child playing with matches. "How *can* you be so disrespectful!" he said. "I wouldn't have thought if of you, Emma."

Emma was bewildered. "What do you mean, disrespectful?"

"An image is a map," Sanctus said. "And we map *people* and *parts* of people for only the most concrete, practical reasons. Healers map a specific person's hand in order to designate an injury. We map generic human bodies and their parts to help us understand how they work. But we *don't* map specific persons' bodies because we desire them, or to make aesthetic objects of them." Sanctus Geloso's eyes froze her with disapprobation. "If your parents didn't teach you manners, surely you had ethics, if not art classes, in your village?"

Though he was a couple of years older, Emma had regarded him as a friend. The sharpness of his attack took her utterly by surprise. Emma's sight blurred with tears; she swallowed convulsively three or four times. All of that stuff was so dry, and it hadn't seemed of any concern to her— or indeed to anyone in the village. They weren't artists, they were all very practical people. Yes, of course she understood about drawing, about how a sketch was a map that highlighted certain kinds of information but never attempted to represent the whole, since the whole of a thing could never be adequately represented in any way shape or form except as aspects of it conformed to classes and subclasses of orders. But drawing Viola Knight's hand— *doodling*— hadn't felt like mapping or attempting a representation, exactly. . . . She had done it without thinking, compulsively— a response, really, to the way that image was always with her.

Emma got her tears under control. She began to feel angry at being so grievously misunderstood. She said, "Sanctus Geloso, you don't understand! I was drawing an image that evokes something of how I feel about Viola Knight. I wasn't trying to represent *her*."

"Just your *feelings* for her?" Sanctus said— looking and sounding scathingly skeptical. "Trying to pin down what it is that so excites you about her, is that it?"

"No!" Emma said. "That's not it! It's more like an evocation. Only I'm not an artist, so I can't do it with any sophistication!"

"No ethical artist would *ever* evoke a person by drawing a part of their body," Sanctus said severely. "Any more than an actor would pretend to be representing a human being. Think about it, Emma. The map isn't the object it denotes. With nonhuman objects, that's pretty easy to remember, and when one confuses the map with a nonhuman object, one generally makes a fool of oneself. With persons, though, it's the other way around. When one maps a human, he or she almost instantly conforms to the map, for it becomes what you and others notice about that person. Which is why most people in the world have long since concluded that drawing a map of someone is disrespectful."

Emma thought ruefully of the subtleties of the play she had seen and the group's discussion of it. It had been *all* evocation, which was trickier in drama than in fiction or sculpture or painting, precisely because of the difficulty of making sense while avoiding mapping personalities. The actor's and dramatist's arts were the trickiest. The entire group agreed about *that*. Emma said, "I suppose you're right, Sanctus. But I'm so. . .*obsessed*. I keep seeing her hand in my mind. And so my fingers just keep wanting to draw it. As though it's imprinted on my brain."

Sanctus pursed his full, shapely lips. "Sexual love is so uncivilized," he said. "We never see the object of our love except in really skewed, perverse ways. I suppose one could say that falling in love is like inscribing a map on one's vision. There's just the map, and everything that isn't on it is meaningless." Sanctus sighed. "Have a care for what you're doing, Emma. If you start one little bit of human mapping, before you know it you'll be mapping everything, in your mind if not actually on-screen." He tugged his boyishly purple and flame sleeve down over his lanky, ungainly wrist and gave her a knowing look. "It really is a slippery slope. And at the bottom lies not only alienation from civilization, but insanity."

Emma pictured herself on a steep, treeless hill slicked with mud and oil, struggling to keep her footing.

Sanctus said, "Wouldn't it be more honest to get her out of your system with an affair, rather than simply obsessing about her all the time?"

Emma felt too foolish to do more than mumble a noncommittal reply and beat a hasty retreat. Even if she could *map* out her feelings, he still wouldn't understand. That she *knew*.

7.

Emma's pleasure-pain became the nausea of confused bad feelings. Walking through campus to town and then to the very outskirts, Emma Persimmon reviewed moment after moment from her past in which she or another child had been castigated for "characterizing" herself or someone else. *One does not say that Alan Farnseworth is a tattletale. One says that Alan Farnseworth tattled again to the teacher. There's a difference, Emma, a big difference. Only certain kinds of generalizations are honest and respectful, namely those that identify a person in terms of guild affiliation, status, age, and village. But a characterization is a generalization pretending to say everything that's important about a person, when it says only something very partial and is a violation of their integrity. A statement of fact is just that. It's something that allows others to draw their own conclusions, depending on context and history. Remember how terrible you felt when that little girl in your class said you were "moony"?*

But was drawing the hand of one's beloved the same thing? No, Emma decided, it was not. Her drawings of that hand were signs she made for herself alone, not maps that others could read. And if her drawings mapped anything, they mapped her *desire* for Viola, not Viola herself. The distinction was crucial! Emma recalled what Montrose Beckoner had had to say about art, maps, and the gaze just the other day. The gaze was the common way of looking at a thing, what some people might call the *correct* way. If you read the map correctly, you took from it the same information everyone else did. The *correct* information. If you looked at a piece of architecture with what Montrose called "the aesthetic gaze," you saw what the architect intended you to see, what any careful, aesthetically acute observer would see. The *look* was something else. It was *private*. It wasn't shared. It was per-verse— and maybe profane.

And the look usually focused on signs, rather than on maps. Who but Emma Persimmon could know what that wrist bone and out-of-proportion third knuckle were supposed to *mean*?

Emma rushed back to campus, ecstatic. Sanctus Geloso had been wrong to chastise her for dissing the woman of her dreams. He had mistaken her look for the gaze. He had mis-taken her desire for an object desired. He'd been, in short, presumptuous: which made it all his problem, not hers.

8.

A few nights later when Emma arrived home from a re-cital given by Pelagia Compton, the principal master with whom Letitia Shadows studied, she was surprised to find Viola Knight in the bathroom— staring at a narrow patch of Edge that had manifested in the small open space bordered by the walls of basins and stalls. It looked very strange to her there, and for a moment she didn't know why. It seemed to be a green stew of seaweed, heaving with irregular tidal swells over sharp crude craggy bits of rock showing the sheen of pink, violet, and green slime wherever they were exposed. As an Edge, it was, Emma supposed, fairly typical. And yet some-thing about it struck her as not quite right.

"Reminds me of birthing," Viola said. "If we could smell it, I imagine it would be damned rank."

Emma had trouble tearing her eyes away from it— even to look on Viola's freshly scrubbed face. "There's something strange about it," she said.

"Yes," Viola said. "We don't expect to find a Seam appear-ing in the middle of a room, especially one so small as this."

One usually got thin strips along walls free of shelves or furniture. But a solid— albeit small— block, right out in the middle? Of course, if either of them moved into that area, it would be bound to disappear. But. . .Viola, as though musing aloud, said, "Makes me wonder if the conventional wisdom— that the only place major fields can appear are on the ice at the poles and in desert or tundra, might not be correct. Imagine building an enormous empty space enclosed by four walls and just waiting to see if a field appeared." Apparently recalling that Emma was totally ignorant about tachyon fields except for what she'd told her on the walk back to the bus, Viola smiled condescendingly. "You see, it's always been assumed they're random and cannot be systematically studied," she said.

Full of wonder, Emma said, "Do you think the engineering guild would build such a place, if they knew about this appearance?"

Viola, still favoring Emma with that same smile, shrugged. "That's doubtful. They'd have to be able to justify the expenditure. I *suppose* they could simply say they wanted to study tachyons. But it would be risky. Certainly it would put all engineers involved in danger of breaking their oaths."

"Don't you see," Emma said passionately— but had to stop when Eudora Fromm and Gilda Pershing came in, so absorbed in a conversation about avian ethology that they never noticed the odd way Emma and Viola were positioned.

The women crossed into the Edge, causing it to vanish. Presumably it would come back. But since the small bit of Edge that had been in her room at the beginning of the term had vanished the previous week without being replaced by another, Emma felt bereft, anyway.

9.

The Edge in the bathroom did not reappear. Or was it that it had gone and would not return? Thinking, for the first time, about some of the possible implications of the little that Viola had told her about "Seams," Emma Persimmon realized she didn't know whether there was a difference between the perception of an Edge and its actually being there. When one stopped perceiving an Edge— say, when one moved into it, forcing it to retreat, did the field itself— as Viola called it— vanish because it was utterly disrupted, or did it just *seem* to disappear? Though she had long since lost her infantile delight in playing *fort/da*, she had never stopped testing Edges. Usually the Edge did return when one had moved out of it.

As Emma thought up a whole new set of questions about the Edge, she grew disturbed about the loss of that particular Edge in the bathroom— and with Viola Knight, whose attitude she irrationally began to associate with the loss. Viola's apparent obliviousness to her feelings, Viola's certainty in the wisdom of her guild's secrecy, irked her. A sense of grievance swept over her. She took up her old habit of following Viola, but now with a doggedness that was almost angry.

Emma dreamed of bees swarming busily around their hive, lapping up honey almost as fast as they made it. Swooping and buzzing indoors, loaded with nectar she could not deliver, night after night Emma flew into the bright odorless meadow of an Edge, only to smash into the wall, thwarted each time she sought to escape, destined to kill herself trying.

At meals Emma picked desultorily at her food and often lost track of conversations. Her friends thought it a simple case of unconsummated love. But to Emma, there was nothing simple about it, though what wasn't simple she dared not say aloud.

One evening Ledora Fairly drew Emma into her room, to offer her advice and instruction. "Embolden yourself, Emma!" she said. "When you know what you want, you must take it."

Ledora had no furniture except for a drafting table and matching high stool. The walls and ceiling were covered with mirrors and lights. Flinching from her own reflection, Emma thought that only the physical perfection that dancers necessarily embodied would make it possible to live in such an environment, where one could never escape the reality of one's appearance.

Ledora Fairly positioned the stool near the small window. She said, "Please, Emma, sit." Every movement the dancer made suggested extravagance. Even the simplest gesture of arm evoked grace and. . .*immediacy*. As though nothing mattered so much as the *moment*. Emma got a little excited. Dancers were such unpredictable creatures.

Perched on the stool, Emma found her eyes about level with Ledora's. "I'm going to put a personal question to you, Emma," the dancer said. "Answer it or not, but do tell the truth. Are you feeling frustrated in getting Viola Knight's attention?"

Emma almost slid off the stool in embarrassment. She pressed her trembling fingers to her burning cheeks.

"Trailing her like a dog in search of a master is not going to work with a Viola Knight," Ledora said sternly. "Nor will going up to her, tapping her on the shoulder, and telling her you're hot for her bod."

Emma lowered her eyes, wishing she could, like the Edge, vanish on penetration.

"But if you want her, you can get her, and I can show you how."

Ledora made it simple, when it wasn't. But tired of smashing into walls keeping her from the heavenly honey of the hive, Emma took Simple, and went for it.

10.

Haunted with desire and verging on anger with the object of that desire, the shy and retiring Ms. Persimmon now flagrantly flaunted it. If she had thought she was being obvious wearing a red scarf, she now added red gloves, stockings, and broad-brimmed hat to her person. And instead of following Viola Knight, Emma anticipated her— popping up several times a day just where Viola was about to be. Though she could not be as immediate as a dancer, Emma became more immediate than she would ever have imagined possible. Emma buzzed furiously in pursuit of The Moment.

Viola noticed. Oh yes. But swept up in the dry elegance of partial differential equations, she found it easy to procrastinate anything that was a distraction from her own agenda. It was only on the Saturday afternoon when she found the reddest of red Emmas awaiting her as she got off the bus at the edge of town that she understood she would not be able to ignore such passion so much as a split-second longer.

"Emma, let's walk," she said, prepared to be stern and firm with her pursuer. But the Moment positively ambushed her as she perceived through all her senses the vivid, intense, now-ness of Emma Persimmon's desire. The brilliance of Emma's gaze drove scalding waves of sensation through her bones and sinews, and the radiance of Emma's expression dazzled her, damping her awareness of the rest of the world. In that moment only Emma and Emma's passion existed. Viola's nerves sang. Her belly and thighs grew heated and heavy. Now visible in all its splendor, Emma's desire threatened to possess her whole.

When they had gotten well into the woods, out of sight of the bus, they stopped, and Viola touched Emma's cheek. "Emma, all this beauty. I'm overwhelmed! But— for *me?*"

Emma closed her eyes at the thrill of that touch. She perceived that her beloved was moved, rendered almost too breathless to speak. And yet the warning in Viola's voice, the tone that told Emma that Viola, though excited, was grudging, did not escape her notice. Emma laid her hand over Viola's; her lips addressed the hard, callused palm, her tongue the sharp little knob of bone on the wrist, with her answer.

Viola murmured pleasure, piquing Emma's pricked ears. But— "Emma," she said. "You must understand, my passion is physics. Which demands all I've got. I've sworn off romance and will marry only engineers. Physics is my life, it owns me!"

Feeling her power, Emma grew bold, yes, and let her desire soar and carry her where it would. They might no longer have been in the stark winter forest, they might be aflutter in the hot desert Edge, like shimmering hummingbirds dipping their long pointed beaks into the soft mauve bells of willows, sipping nectar, dripping pollen, shifting only for another beakfull. Their palms and fingers and lips laid trails, cunning and lingual. The Moment was all Emma had ever hoped for.

"You can have us both," Emma said when she had breath to speak, breath all full of the scent of Viola.

Viola's body had loosened, sensation all slipping and sliding in an abandon that set her wanting wanting wanting all that Emma's hands and lips were promising. "I can't, I can't," she whispered— even as she was discovering the fine-haired neck so eager and responsive under Emma's scarlet silk scarf.

The Moment was bliss, but yielded to struggle. Emma's passion equaled Viola's will. Their pleasure was so outrageous and breathless Emma knew they must be Fated Lovers. But Viola swore it was a once-and-only-once kind of thing. She had been tempted to infidelity and had been weak. It would not, she said, ever happen again.

Emma could not believe it. It made her numb, hearing passion put into the past tense, even as the tingle was still receding from her thighs and buttocks. It defied nature! Could Physics, she wondered, be so perverse? Suddenly she saw the forest around her— gray, damp, and stark. The chill bit at her skin as she pulled herself up to glare down at Viola. This is what it feels like to be a woman, she thought. For after the Moment comes knowledge.

She said, "Listen to me, listen to me, Viola Knight. If it weren't for passion, I would be hating you. You are wrong to try to keep yourself cold for your work, and you are wrong, wrong, wrong to conceal the existence of the Edge. Your attitude sucks, big-time. And pretending to be above feeling is sick."

Viola sat up, too. She leaned close to brush bits of twigs and leaves from Emma's hair with an attitude of intimacy that nearly melted Emma's insistence. She handed Emma the bright fleecy hat that had come off in their wildest and sweetest of moments, then leaned close again, meaning, Emma was sure, to kiss her. But Viola suddenly reared back. Her breath hissed in sharply; her eyelashes fluttered. She scooted back a few inches, snatched up her sweater, and pulled it quickly over her head. "What silly things are you saying, Emma? You talk like an irresponsible child!"

Viola's voice was taunting. She took her cloak from the ground and wrapped it tightly around herself. "Until we have exact knowledge of what the fields are and how to map them it's a certainty that people will behave stupidly and make up every sort of nonsense about them on which to base religions and start wars all over again. Must we have war again, just to make the rare individuals like yourself secure in their sense of reality?"

The tone of Viola's voice nicked Emma's heart like a knife so cold it felt hot in her breast. Bitterly she pulled on her pants and wished her hat were any color but red. "Why must there always be a common gaze for perceiving anything that's represented?" She tugged her flame red socks into place. "Why must the existence of something inexplicable and ineffably different make people want to claim they know what it is?" She felt so angry with Viola she had to bury her fists in her cloak to keep from hitting her. "And why can't we tolerate private, individual looking, instead of insisting always on The Gaze?"

Viola had no idea what Emma was talking about. *Her* friends never discussed such things. Maps, to her, were constructs for understanding physical reality. They certainly weren't territories to be fought over. She said, "I want to be an engineer. More than anything. And yes, more than being a lover, Emma. And keeping quiet about something that is of concern to you— but maybe to no one else in the world— is a price I'm willing to pay."

Angry, sad, crying, Emma watched Viola finish dressing. When Viola stood quickly, without warning, Emma clutched Viola's legs in a panic. "Don't go yet," she said, openly pleading. "Don't go. I understand, really I do. But don't you think it's at all. . .*wrong?*"

Viola looked down at her. It seemed to Emma that she had already, in her heart, gone. "Would it matter, Emma, if I did?"

Emma rushed into her sweater and scrambled to her feet. "Of course it would," she said. "Of course it would matter." She blinked to clear her eyes of tears. "Couldn't you at least think about trying— later, when you're a master— changing the rules of your guild? Couldn't you at least think about the negative consequences of your silence?"

Viola kissed Emma's nose lightly. "Of course I can. And I will. But you just remember, too, that without my guild, I don't exist. And if I spoke openly about Seams, the rest of the world would say I was crazy, and what good would that do anyone?"

"There's got to be a way," Emma said fiercely. "I know there has!"

A silence sprang up between them. It grew charged and heavy. Viola swallowed and cleared her throat. "Before I go back to town, I want to check to see if there's a Seam in that place now." Her voice was hoarse and shaky.

Defiantly, Emma took Viola's arm, making it clear she intended to accompany her.

Viola's face flamed. She backed hastily away. She was back in the Moment, whatever she might say.

Emma smiled lovingly, in utter sureness of her power. A woman now, she knew her own strength.

Arms linked, breaths steaming in the cold, they set out together— lovers of the Moment— for the Edge.

The Gift

1.

"I don't know what bug's gotten up your ass," Stavros said when he saw the new piece. "But your choice of words is bound to piss off all those tourists who might find the penitential ritual fascinating and gross out all the rest. GTI would bounce it if I sent it to them as is."

Florentine couldn't remember the last time Stavros had asked her to make changes in a piece. But she knew he was right. The section in question featured a stand-up in the Plaza of Penitence, with her POV showing some poor down-in-the-mouth slob creeping on bleeding hands into the Plaza, his nose a virtual geyser of blood. Her voice-over ran:

Blue Downs is the kind of place where you're likely to see people crawling on their hands and knees down the main drag a couple of days a week. Many tourists will, I'm sure, find this a fascinating, even thrilling sight. I found it irritating in the extreme, myself, to the point of being tempted to join those who take righteous civic pleasure in kicking the damned fools and otherwise jeering them on their way, but for my far more powerful urge to kick those doing the kicking. Blue Downs suffers a raging thirst for public humiliation of its truants, miscreants, and trespassers, a thirst no amount of sleazy quaffing can slake. For that reason alone I'd rate the penitential ritual as one of the most significant characteristics of this city, however widely known Blue Downs is for the superior graphic arts displayed in its churches, market district, and more affluent homes.

Galactic Tours, Inc., made a bundle off Florentine's travelogues and always paid her well in the expectation that every piece she produced would bring the big spenders running. But she knew that Stavros was probably right when he warned that they wouldn't see the point of her presenting a "darker view" of a city known for its cultural brilliance. As he put it, "That kind of thing is fine for pieces on places known for their sin and sleaze. But Blue Downs practically stands for purity of spirit in an atmosphere of high corporate profit."

Fixing the piece would be easy: splice in an old bit on the lack of beggars, pushers, and prostitutes in the street; remove all references to penitential exercises; and dig through her files for fully sunlit rather than shadowed shots, which she'd favored throughout. She wouldn't, though, delete any of the material about the Blue Downs musical scene. Stavros agreed that all of that was "interesting, if a bit disturbing." Absent any reference to the penitents, it shouldn't have the "sullying effect" he apparently feared could dim the city's lustrous reputation for purity.

That reputation now seriously galled Florentine. If she could, she'd let the rest of the galaxy in on the secret. "The Custodian of Human Arts," Big Blue was usually called, and many people considered it simply one grand all-encompassing museum.

Oh Alain, my Alain. My heart, my love. My loss.

Florentine found her loss an unbearably lonely one. How could anyone who didn't really know Blue Downs ever understand? And how could she burden even one of the few souls she could confidently call *friend* with the story of such a loss? Time-dilation was the mother of discretion. Florentine's every friend traveled, too. A momentous change in their lives never failed to break apart old friendships, which, depending on an even, smooth semblance of continuity for their long-term maintenance, could not sustain major upheaval. Worse, she knew that the story of her loss would make sense to no one to whom what happened to her might matter. *How could you have been so foolish?* she could already hear any possible listener say. Merely telling the story— unless she told it lightly, ironically, as a little cautionary tale at her own expense— would have exposed her to the charge of *whining*.

Some day, no doubt, she would discover and appreciate the irony in her story. But that day lay so far in her subjective future that she found it difficult to believe in.

2.

When Stavros had said he thought it was about time for Florentine to do another tour of Blue Downs and reminded her that GTI had said it would finance as many tours of the place as she cared to produce, her initial reaction was *been there, done that*, maximum yawn. Her Blue Downs tours were top sellers that appealed especially to people who had never before traveled. GTI liked this attractiveness to an audience of non-travelers because her pieces on Blue Downs tended to draw a significant number of them into taking the tour. GTI also liked the numbers showing that each time Florentine made an additional tour of a place she'd previously covered, a significant number of travelers who had done the previous tour signed up for the new one. Stavros worked on the basis of royalties rather than fees; not surprisingly, his advice typically addressed the bottom line.

Blue Downs had always been special for Florentine; it had launched her travelogue career, and she counted the day GTI accepted her first proposal to tour that city as one of the most exciting moments of her life. It had been shortly after that that Stavros, though he professed to be gloomy with the conviction that Florentine was likely to fail since her knowledge of Blue Downs was strictly academic and her life experience "almost nil," contracted to be her agent. His attitude had only spurred her determination to bring her academic love for Blue

Downs into her work, to seduce all who viewed the tour with every tone and nuance of its many and wondrous beauties. And Florentine's first two visits to Blue Downs in the flesh had in fact consummated her adoration— more profoundly the second time even than the first.

She hadn't had the faintest idea that she had grown jaded with the very idea of Blue Downs until Stavros suggested the third tour. Hearing herself tell him *been there, done that* shocked her as much as it amused him. Looking back, she supposed that that reaction must have been an effect of her having done so very many tours around the galaxy for GTI— or an effect of age.

Still, months after Stavros had first made the suggestion, as she prepared to leave the starship to shuttle down to the surface of Big Blue, she enjoyed a pleasant sense of anticipating known delights and meeting up with company already proven to be comfortably congenial. The feeling held even through the unpleasant shuttle flight and surged when she stepped out onto the planet's surface, reeling with fatigue and the lingering traces of nausea.

Her positive mood dissipated, though, and just the slightest undercurrent of something griped her— not cynicism, not boredom, and certainly not anxiety— when she found Magdalene awaiting her as she exited the shuttleport's Public Safety intake center.

They kissed one another twice on both cheeks in the grand Blue Downs style and frankly examined the marks of age and other changes on one another's faces. Florentine hadn't expected Magdalene to meet her; she hadn't even let Magdalene know that she was coming. She told herself that she should feel flattered to be met, but instead felt nagged and stifled even before Magdalene told her she had reserved a suite for Florentine at one of the more elaborate B&Bs, where she had on her previous visit agreed— in theory— that she should stay her next time in Blue Downs. GTI had, as usual, reserved palatial quarters for Florentine in one of the city's most luxe hotels. Florentine knew enough about Blue Downs mores to take this presumption— like her meeting Florentine before she'd had a chance to recover from the grueling shuttle trip and decon— as a gesture of warm affection. And so she smiled widely and thanked Magdalene for the intended courtesy. Why not stay at the B&B, she thought as the undercurrent erupted into something verging on recklessness. Why not make this tour something off the beaten path. She could still take up the aesthetic delicacies due to be featured in tour number three. But she could also include a few touches of "local color" while she was at it— something more than the charming interview with the master glassblower in tour number two; not anything "folksy" or anthropological, but something revealing the apparently sophisticated though largely unexamined personality and character of Blue Downs itself— something that would show Blue Downs as more than a mere repository for brilliant fine and applied arts.

Magdalene was apparently little better off financially than she had been in her student days, when Florentine had last seen her, for she said, when Florentine introduced the subject of transport, that she had trained out to the shuttleport. Her eyes lit up when Florentine said that GTI had arranged to lease an air car with driver. "It so reminds me of when you were last here," she said, almost sighing. "It makes me nostalgic for those days, which I've thought about so often, you know."

The expression in her eyes— gleaming, melting, wistful— made Florentine uncomfortably aware of how differently they regarded the "old times" they had shared. Florentine could see that for Magdalene they had been a taste of glamour and sophistication, furnished by all the fine dining and first-class theater tickets Florentine had at her disposal and spiced by tales of her galactic travels. For Florentine, though, it had been the delight of a set of young companions— Magdalene among several— open to experiencing all that they could, loathing cliché, engaged and intelligent and fresh: a pleasant interval, in retrospect, recalled only in fragments and therefore lacking the cohesion of emotional significance.

Florentine enjoyed the aerial view of Big Blue as greatly as she had the first time she had seen it. Sky, water, and grass glistened in every shade of blue imaginable. Across the 100 kilometers that lay between the shuttleport and Blue Downs rolled softly mounded hills that made her think of velvet and silk and jewelers' display windows. "It still doesn't look real to me," she said to Magdalene.

"You used to say that nothing about Blue Downs ever felt real to you," Magdalene replied.

"True." Florentine suppressed a surge of irritation at the reminder. She knew that Magdalene was only being polite and friendly in letting her know how much she remembered of those old days. But she detested any suggestion of sentimentality from someone who really only barely knew her.

Since Florentine had reviewed Magdalene's most recent communication to her shortly before boarding the shuttle, she was able to ask the right sorts of questions about her family and work life and so occupy the remaining conversational space until their arrival in Blue Downs. Though she no longer found Magdalene's eagerness charming and delightful, she had no difficulty keeping their interaction running smoothly. Magdalene, never having traveled off Big Blue, could have no notion of the effort this cost Florentine. Tired to death with the exigencies of travel, Florentine was eager to bathe and desperate to sleep. But this she managed, somehow, to conceal from Magdalene.

3.

That first afternoon Florentine sent Magdalene away with the promise that they'd meet for lunch the next day and the remark that she was interested in getting into more of the music scene than the concert attendance of her previous tours.

Magdalene's son, she knew, was a concert-vocalist. He seemed the logical way in to an area of Blue Downs society previously inaccessible to her.

Big Blue was one of those fortunate worlds where water was abundant, and the B&B, as luxe as any of Blue Downs' hotels, included a large whirlpool bath in its accommodations. That first evening Florentine spent more than an hour in the tub as she considered her plan to make full use of Magdalene's local insights and connections. Florentine felt confident that Magdalene would enjoy being used— enjoy alternating the role of guide with that of sidekick, enjoy introducing her family and friends to someone she thought of as "famous."

Florentine went to bed early that night and slept an opaque, heavy fourteen hours. Despite the enormous physical fatigue from the shuttle trip and the additional stress on her body of diurnal-phase adjusters, she woke full of energy and ready, if not eager, to take on the challenge of making the stale fresh. Her outlook that morning as she went down to the breakfast room was strictly professional. She sampled and evaluated the B&B's morning cuisine in full work mode, with nothing more on her mind than making this third tour the most interesting yet of her pieces. Though she did not always include in her travelogues reports on all the places at which she ate, GTI paid her a fixed fee per meal reported separately (with a maximum of two meals per restaurant), since they used such reports in their accommodations directories.

After breakfast she wandered about the market district recording pieces of public art not covered in her previous tours. Magdalene had arranged to meet her at exactly one hour after noon, for what in Blue Downs culture was the main meal of the day. At the time of making the arrangements she had also informed Florentine that she would have a particularly interesting surprise for her there. In many places in the galaxy, "surprises" are not polite and are usually unwelcome. No doubt it was the prospect of a surprise that made Florentine grumble (silently) about badly named restaurants as she approached the Singing Orchard at the time appointed.

Her bad mood vanished the instant she set foot inside the restaurant. The entire place, a full square city block, was apparently open-air and thus basked under the constantly cobalt sky that granted the clarity and crispness of vision the planet, with its slightly oxygen-thin mixture of air, was famous for. A cool, moist breeze carried the scents of the fruit adorning the orchard's many trees and wafted tantalizing snatches of music unlike anything Florentine had ever before heard. She fell, almost at once, under a spell of enchantment. (How else explain what followed, except by reference to the most ancient of fairy tales?) Standing just inside the entrance, she abandoned herself so entirely to her senses that the Maitre d' had to speak sharply to get her attention.

A robotic cart carried her through the trees to the table where Magdalene had already been seated. Clear cermet platforms, elevated perhaps two meters off the ground, were set discreetly among the trees. At the horizon Florentine made out a succession of the city's splendid bell towers, which she had no trouble identifying— first that of the Church of Christ the Redeemer, followed by those of the Jesus Died Christian Church, Holy Cross Catholic Church, The Church of Repentance, the Church of Mount Olives, Holy Spirit Pentecostal, Make A Joyful Noise unto the Lord Church of Christ— at which point Florentine halted her identifications. She knew that they couldn't all be simultaneously visible. The bell towers must, she thought, be magnificent holographs.

Which made her wonder, for a moment, whether any of the trees were real.

Magdalene waved gaily down at Florentine from one of the elevated platforms, and the cart halted. As the platform lowered slowly to ground level, Florentine waded through a shallow sea of ferns, lichen, and ivy to the nearest tree— a relatively lofty pear— and touched its trunk. It had to be real. Its bark scraped her knuckles when she knocked on it.

The platform waited as Florentine finished checking out more of the trees. (All were real.) When she had finally seated herself and the platform began its ascent, the table informed the women that though the menu at the Singing Orchard varied daily, it was fixed, assembled in accord with the finest Matrix Aesthetics principles, ensuring that the component parts of the meal achieved a unique aesthetic experience beyond their mere sum. Typically, the table said, even the best restaurants concentrated their efforts on providing very fine components without regard for their total aesthetic effect. The art of the Singing Orchard, it assured them, did not aim so low.

Her eyes brimming with excitement and mirth, Magdalene watched Florentine closely. Florentine knew, even then, that this visit to the Singing Orchard would probably be the centerpiece of the tour. She had discussed Matrix Aesthetics in both of her previous tours but had always concentrated on its architectural and graphic exemplars. It had never occurred to her that the pleasures of the palate, throat, and gut could fall under its sway, too.

The service began not with the customary Blue Downs bread, but with a few morsels of a sweetly tender, spiced shellfish over which a thin, tartly fruited sauce had been drizzled. A half-glass of a very dry wine with a delicate pear aftertaste accompanied this dish, which was followed immediately by long slivers of avocado, red pepper, and snow peas dressed with a cumin-pecan vinaigrette. The shapes, textures, colors, and play of light in the two arrangements offered as much a feast for the eyes as the flavors provided a piquant delight to the palate. *Then* came the bread, a small round that could be eaten in a single bite, fragrantly warm and textured and crusty.

The music arrived with the shellfish, along with a wash of light and shadows that played in the leaves and fruit of the trees surrounding them. Though Florentine's implant recorded the mix of sound and visual images during the meal, she later found that the recording proved inadequate to the experience for the simple reason that it recorded only what she directly focused on— which could not be the whole, but merely the components, superb as they were.

So many subtle, not-fully-perceived sensory inputs surrounded and overwhelmed her with ecstatic sensations that she thought that only sexual orgasm could begin to approximate such physical and emotional intensity. The cuisine itself included many, many courses of maddeningly small portions, each teasing and flattering her palate, piquing her appetite— with increasingly longer intervals between courses. After only a few of the innumerable courses, she began to feel suspended outside the time-space continuum. Soon her entire body grew inflamed with the longing to gorge on any one of the excellent dishes set before her. Gorging, at least, would have given her the satisfaction of bludgeoning into submission so much that was elusive. Set outside time, overstimulated by an abundance of sensory inputs, she couldn't help but compare it to extended sexual foreplay— and began, finally, to wonder (almost anxiously!) whether, at the rate they were teasing her carnal desires, she would ever attain climax and satiation. Still, however maddening she found the experience, she never ceased to be thrilled by the awareness that she had never before been so overtaken by perfection and beauty— and would probably never be again.

Neither of the women used words for the duration of the meal. They exchanged speaking glances that acknowledged a shared— though separate— pleasure; but neither could bear to interrupt such beauty with the all too ordinary and banal blather of their own speech. Several times, glimpsing a certain expression in Magdalene's eyes, Florentine recollected memories of a Magdalene thirty years younger caught up in moments of wondrously naive pleasure that Florentine herself had long since forgotten. Yet for all the intensity of her pleasure, Florentine never once lost her professional awareness, which analyzed and intellectually appreciated the aesthetics of the experience in a way that heightened her sensual pleasure.

Her greatest delight— even greater than that of the palate, though the whole was indeed beyond the sum of its magnificent parts— fell in the realm of the aural. During the initial courses the music— which she at first thought wholly instrumental and canned— seemed to emanate from the trees, which she assumed held the speakers that were presumably disseminating it. But as they sipped a fiery gazpacho, a movement glimpsed over Magdalene's shoulder caught and drew Florentine's eye to the silvery shimmer of an olive tree a few yards from the base of the platform, where she spotted the first of the singers that she soon discovered were surrounding them (arranged, naturally, according to some arcane principle of Matrix Aesthetics). Perhaps it was the influence of Blue Downs working on her imagination, but in that first moment he looked to Florentine exactly like the incarnation of a depiction of an angel such as could be found in any of the city's churches. He stood— quite deliberately, without doubt, given the operation of the matrix— in a pool of sunlight, a muscular blond Adonis with a powerful diaphragm and magnificent posture that looked as though it could easily support a pair of wings should they have suddenly been inspired to sprout from his back. His voice soared powerfully, its tone rich and buttery, even as it sliced through the air as cleanly and purely as a polished and honed silver blade might cleave a block of hard, crystalline ice.

Infatuation, fascination, obsession teased and tempted her. And yet, what she felt wasn't simply lust— anymore than her appreciation of the meal's aesthetics was driven simply by gluttony. A grandly aspiring, yearning emotion suffused her, filling her with elation that such joy-in-fleshliness even existed. Never had she so appreciated the embodiedness of humanity, never had she so recognized the power that lay in that aspect of human existence— as opposed to the unending, crude efforts humans collectively put forward their every conscious (and unconscious) moment to transcend the animal status that their every cultural and intellectual achievement sought to deny.

Ecstatic, she felt she had achieved the single most perfect moment possible for someone lacking the extraordinary talents and abilities that only artists and athletes were given to know. The ecstasy became nearly unbearable when that moment continued long past what she felt she could sustain. It came as an unexpected relief, then, when this near-angel stepped into shadow and fell silent and a new moment of wonder took hold of her.

The musicians also included instrumentalists. Though the lot of them shifted position throughout the meal, they remained always around the women, a sonic matrix that integrated perfectly with the food and light and images. Even during the silences interpolating the music, Florentine's ears registered a pressure, a presence surrounding and impacting her much in the same way the intervals between courses did. Later, she learned that the matrices were overlapping, conceptualized as sited on intersecting planes. "The visible and audible," her informant would tell her, "is contingent on a layer of inaudibility and invisibility, which it makes present as a certain absence." Every aesthetic experience, he claimed, depended on something that was never directly perceived, an axis grounding all perception and cognition. In Matrix Aesthetics, the artists were not only conscious of this imperceptible axis, but deliberately determined its location, whether for subtle or maximum effects.

Some of the time Florentine felt as though the meal were taking an eternity, and she had the thought that one would never be able to bear an eternity of bliss, even as she lingered at the edge of exhaustion and overstimulation and being tired of not being *full*, not being *finished* with an experience and intensity that must, must, must have limits. Interestingly, it was at the very moment she was thinking about the human need for limits that the denouement suddenly arrived.

Florentine was looking at the fleshly angel as aware of his physical presence as she was of the food when the table presented them with a serving so large, of food so filling, that eating a mere fraction of it made Florentine's stomach ache with the wickedly wonderful pain of gluttony.

She gave up on the food after five chewy, satisfying bites, as though her body suddenly recognized that it had consumed more than an entire day's allowance of alimentation. She wasn't in the least surprised when the table removed their plates and replaced them with small bowls of brilliantly colored and artfully carved ices gaily festooned with small, delicate flowers complemented by ethereally light and frothily aerial music. Her gaze met Magdalene's in a smile both content and gratified— as though they had proven their mettle in a test of their endurance, wits, and taste and not simply been passively receptive of this orchard's aesthetic bounty. Blue Downs' sky never looked so blue to Florentine, its air so pure as it did in that moment.

This odd sense of triumph— which she suspected must be in some way deliberately cultivated as the appropriate emotion with which to finish such an indescribable experience— prevented her from feeling any sort of post-coital *triste* as the platform descended and a robotic cart arrived to remove the women from paradise.

"Well?" Magdalene asked after Florentine had thumbprinted the voucher demanding a small fortune for the afternoon's pleasure and they stepped back into the city. Florentine exulted in the thought of GTI's paying such a price, which by itself exceeded the entire cost of her last tour on the relatively cheap planet of Siliconia. The priciness alone would be enough to make the backwater wealthy who aspired to the heights of Taste swarm into Blue Downs determined to claim the very best (and most expensive meal) their riches could buy. And GTI would certainly have no trouble cutting a lucrative deal for adding the Singing Orchard to its Exclusive

Private Listing. Magdalene touched Florentine's arm. "Have you ever experienced such a meal before in your life?"

This touch on her arm, this explicit demand that they speak without time to reflect about the ineffable, grated on Florentine, abrading the pleasurable aftertaste and the sense of having experienced a delight few people in the galaxy would ever be privileged to know. She had enjoyed sharing the experience with Magdalene, who had surely appreciated it at least as fully (and perhaps even more) than herself, and who had never once throughout the meal said or done anything likely to break the wonderful spell. And yet Florentine found herself resenting Magdalene for intruding on what felt private. Florentine knew her reaction was unwarranted. Certainly she would never have wanted to partake of such a meal alone, for dining at the Singing Orchard without a companion would have been tantamount to masturbating in public.

Florentine barely tolerated the brief touch on her arm; unable to look at the other woman, she kept her gaze straight before her. "The Singing Orchard is unique," she said shortly, hoping that would satisfy the other woman. Why, why, why, she wondered, must people insist on simplifying and degrading an experience with words before it's properly been allowed its due? People often did that with sex, wanting to make a running mutual commendation as though there couldn't possibly be any pleasure in it but that expressed in words, which always, to Florentine's mind, cheapened the pleasure and stripped the embodiedness of the experience to render it abstract and thus lessen its power.

Magdalene said, quickly, "I need to be heading back to the studio now. But I wanted to tell you that my son is meeting with a few other musicians tonight at the Cafe Bellona and said you would be welcome to join them if you liked."

At the moment, all Florentine wanted was some time alone, to digest the meal in peace. But professional sense dictated that she seize on an invitation that might not be offered another time, and so they parted with the understanding that they would meet again in only a few hours.

As Florentine strode rapidly through the streets, her senses nearly closed to the world about her, she thought how sad it was that she now found herself resenting having shared such an experience with Magdalene. The rest of the afternoon passed slowly, uncomfortably, even anxiously. Florentine felt guilty for her resentment and annoyed at herself for the shadow this resentment cast on the meal. But though her resentment made her feel like a creep, she could not shake the belief that she was justified in not wanting to reduce something so wonderful to mere, banal *words*.

4.

The Cafe Bellona looked exactly as it had the last time Florentine had been there. The popular music it used for background sounded harsher to her ear, but in fact it was simply an evolution of the old music, no darker or angrier or more angst-ridden than its antecedents. In planet years the place was three decades older, but for Florentine, its clientele, style of decor, and edginess remained the same. Sometimes, she thought, time dilation didn't matter at all.

But seeing Magdalene in this setting, her eye now perceived that *she* had altered greatly, for Magdalene no longer looked as if she really belonged there. In the few hours since they'd parted, Magdalene had changed into slinky silky lounge-wear and acquired shiny beads and very thin ribboned braids in her hair, numerous earrings and bracelets, and interesting face paint; but something about her looked out of place, as though she were a seeker trying too obviously hard to surface.

Florentine had no trouble spotting her in the jam of close to a hundred vibrating, socializing bodies. Before she could get a good look at the other people squeezed around Magdalene's table, the two of them kissed in the Blue Downs fashion and asked one another the ritual questions of greeting. When they finished, and Florentine glanced around at the others as Magdalene launched into introductions, she saw that the singer in the Orchard, the one who had made her body burn— the one whose back and shoulders looked as if they could carry a magnificent pair of wings effortlessly— was present. Caught in the blur of a total body flush, Florentine missed all the other introductions, but did not miss *his* name— though she *was* sufficiently distracted that she didn't at first match her angel with the Alain she knew to be Magdalene's musician son.

Up close, Florentine saw that his angel-like form was in every way earthy and sensual rather than ethereal. She was suddenly reminded of Magdalene's former warmth and sensuality— recalling how the younger Magdalene had always pressed herself close, had lain whenever she could with her head in Florentine's lap, had twined her arm around Florentine's waist, simply because it was her nature to be physically close to anyone for whom she felt the least bit of affection. Florentine realized, then, that this Alain must be her son Alain. Everything about him— even his gaze and speaking voice, as buttery and graceful as his powerful singing voice— seemed tactile in its warmth. His hair reminded her of honey— as Magdalene's used to— while his skin (unlike Magdalene's olive complexion) made her think of peaches— of a wonderfully soft, golden fruit blushed with a pleasing, glowing pink. Looking straight at her, out of his appraising yet caressing green eyes, his earthiness surrounded Florentine like an embrace, and for a moment it was as though the two of them were the only consciousnesses inhabiting the known universe.

"My mother talks often about your earlier visit to Blue Downs," he said, and Florentine observed that sometimes time dilation did make a difference.

Caught up in the fascination of Alain's presence, Florentine missed the first bits of general conversation and only tuned in when Alain spoke, to tell her that if she was interested, they could show her the "score" for the meal that afternoon at the Singing Orchard. This "score" included not only the notation of the music that had been performed during the meal but also a choreography of the musicians' placement and the visuals, and of course, the cuisine itself.

"Do you understand the basic operating principles of Matrix Aesthetics?" asked Souhlema, who was seated on Alain's immediate right.

"I know it as a philosophy of art." Florentine sipped the thick, fragrant liqueur everyone drank at the Cafe Bellona. "My impression is that there are only two basic principles — the first that form is the matrix of creativity and the second that the deliberate production of matrices generates the maximum possibility for artistic expression." She had that straight out of Rudinov, the basic art history text for interpreting the art of Blue Downs. She had laid these principles out in the first chapter of her thesis, so many years past; and more recently— namely not long after parting from Magdalene that afternoon— she had brushed up on Matrix theory, precisely so that she would be ready to make intelligent conversation with these musicians.

"The notation of the music is only of its fundamental structure and does not denote a specific execution," Jarrow, seated on Alain's immediate left, said.

"The most obvious difference, in Matrix Aesthetics, is what is left out," Alain said, drawing Florentine's eyes to his soft, plush, stunningly shapely lips.

Jarrow said, "In the case of the performance this afternoon, the extradiegetic element was a poem, which only the performers could hear read, a driving, physical presence to us that was an inaudible— but felt— element for *you*."

"What was the poem?" Florentine asked to take her mind off the element of *Alain's* all too driving, physical presence.

Souhlema answered. "A particularly hard piece of rhythmic poetry by Sark Ali, titled *Why don't you see what you're looking at straight on, Brother Jonas?*, the performance of which lasted twenty-five minutes and was repeated exactly four times at carefully spaced intervals."

Everything about Souhlema grated on Florentine's nerves. But then she was wanting badly, even then, to get Alain away so that she could have him and his attention all to herself.

Jarrow leaned most of the way across the table, as though anxious to make sure Florentine could hear him in the general hubbub of the cafe. She found him physically peculiar— his features oddly, disproportionately large, his hands and wrists strangely doughy, looking as if they were made of flesh that had been denied the infrastructure of bone. "Matrix theory is an extrapolation of the old theory that in every act of vision there remains something unseen, the invisibility of which is required to make an objectively real world that exists independent of perception and cognition possible." While Alain's voice was buttery, Jarrow's had the thick, smooth texture of syrup. Jarrow, like Alain, was a singer. Both Souhlema and Joseph, a brooding, depressed type, were percussionists. All four of them had been in the group that had performed that afternoon at the Singing Orchard.

Florentine undertook to play the devil's advocate. She needed some argument for her piece, and this scene in the cafe would provide some Bohemian color that would go a long way to amusing those viewers who would be bored or confused by the discussion itself. Careful not to look at Alain, she smiled at Jarrow and said, "But isn't the so-called missing element— in this case the poem you mention— inessential? One might almost call its offstage recitation an affectation, given its lack of overall importance."

Alain answered before Jarrow could get one word in. His eyes gleamed with excitement, and his voice grew thick with passion even as it soared with exuberance. "Surely you know that the missing element is an essential factor in the visual works produced through Matrix Aesthetics! The final product excludes this element, but in every case the excluded element has helped to determine the final product. Can you begin to imagine what it is like to make music while a piece of rhythmic poetry is beating hard into one's ears?"

Florentine said, "Like trying to make music while sitting in this cafe, maybe?" And she smiled a little wryly at her consciousness that she wasn't as tolerant of a loud musical ambience as she had once been.

Though she hadn't intended it, Florentine wasn't surprised when this remark led Souhlema and Jarrow into a certain kind of earnestly "playful" discussion of how art in general and music in particular was contingent on its definition and production of context rather than its originating intention. Florentine established an interestingly intense eye-contact with Alain somewhere in the middle of this "playful discussion." Magdalene finally broke into their riff to ask if it weren't possible for Florentine to sample some Matrix production first without and then with the missing element.

Florentine smiled warmly, right into Alain's eyes. "Would it be possible?" she asked him. "Because I'm confident I'd find that both helpful and fascinating."

The musicians assured Florentine that not only would it be possible, but that they were also certain they could arrange for her to be present in the Singing Orchard while they were performing.

"They arranged that for me," Magdalene said. "Contingent on my promise to keep out of sight of the audience."

Florentine realized that Magdalene had some kind of special place with this group, as a sort of a maternal sidekick who routinely hung with them. She was her son's best buddy, too, Florentine decided— and didn't much like the thought.

She told them she definitely wanted to take them up on their offer, and the musicians promised to arrange it. Grateful to be spared any further discussion of Matrix Aesthetics until she was "better informed" on the subject, Florentine settled in to ask the usual sorts of questions. What training had they had? And why had they decided to make music for a living, rather than merely for pleasure? Was it easy to make such a living on Big Blue? And how did a commerce-oriented society such as that which dominated Blue Downs regard professional artists?

The evening passed pleasantly for Florentine and gave her some wonderful material for use in the piece. More interestingly, it made Alain personally and vividly real to her— and made her certain, in her very bones and belly, that he was as attracted to her as she was to him.

Only Magdalene's presence kept Florentine from openly pursuing him. She didn't know how Magdalene would take such a development, but she suspected that the other woman would not like it at all.

5.

Florentine rated sitting in on their gig at the Singing Orchard a smashing success. Her access to the "score" choreographing the performance/meal she watched enhanced her understanding of Matrix Aesthetics enormously as well as provided an interesting ground for thinking about her own experience of such a meal. More importantly, the contact with Alain proved to be the turning point in moving them from amiable acquaintances to passionately engaged. . .not lovers, yet, but something more than friends. Through constantly recurring eye-contact, small touches, and a series of private asides, they established the fact of a powerful mutual attraction, an attraction that Florentine understood Alain was as eager as she to pursue.

Neither of them, of course, were given any food at the Singing Orchard, and Florentine had, in any case, to check out another restaurant for the evening meal, so she invited Alain— and only Alain— to join her. If the other musicians were disappointed, they had the good manners not to show it.

Since it was far too early for supper, Alain agreed to accompany Florentine to one of the smaller churches on her list, one she hadn't seen on her previous visits to Blue Downs. The Church of the One True God sat literally in the shadow of the cathedral. For that reason, perhaps, it made use of only artificial light, something one saw in few pieces of architecture on a planet with the kind of radiance Big Blue's sun bestowed upon it. In the nave and especially over the altar and on the enormous symbol of death hanging over it, narrow shafts of light descended from a lacily ornate strutwork that obscured their sources, as though beamed down straight from heaven. While the nave seemed almost unnaturally still and their footsteps flat and muted though the wood planks they trod were uncarpeted, when one stood in one of these shafts of light, equally thin shafts of music pierced the silence, resonating with an almost eerie spirituality that would have been more suited to corporate glass and marble than the visually warm wood and silk of this church.

Alain stood in one of those flushes of light, his smooth young skin flattered by the illumination, his eyes swimming with pride and pleasure as he listened to the music his presence on that spot had triggered. "Jarrow and I are the singers in this bit," he said. "Ponsonby, whom you haven't met, wrote it." He stopped speaking, and Florentine could feel him listening. Suddenly the light began pulsing with harshly powerful bursts like showers of diamonds, blinding yet rich, that made her vision go dark and then stamped it with dots of colored lights that bounced in patterns she was convinced were deliberately synchronized with the music. The flow of the music itself swelled into a cascade of shimmering sound, sparkling in the brilliance of the moment. Alain, standing motionless in the light, became two-dimensional to Florentine's eyes, like a flat black-and-white photograph in the sharpest focus and of the highest resolution.

And then the moment passed, and Alain stepped out of the light and the music was just music and Alain merely ordinary flesh and blood, and a smile passed between him and

Florentine, a smile of knowledge that would not be spoken, perhaps because it could not be. Then Alain showed her the rest of the church's treasure, and they left. A don't-miss sight, she rated the little church. Later, she thought of it as the place where she and Alain first began to love one another.

6.

Florentine nearly asked Alain to stay that night with her. His warmth and eagerness and her excitement made physical consummation seem inevitable, but in the end, she hesitated at the brink, wary of a gentle but firm reserve in him that she did not feel she understood well enough to risk disregarding. Before meeting Alain, she would have stated, as a fact, that twenty-five-year-old males were invariably shallow and callow and depthless, however socially adept and sophisticated they might be. Alain was different. Though he showed no signs of true depression, she sensed, lurking beneath his warm, easy presentation, a profound, thoroughgoing sadness. This sadness seemed so *natural* to him that she found herself thinking that he must have been born sad and had carried this sadness with him for all the years of his short, talented life. She hadn't known many artists. She thought that perhaps the sadness was linked with his music, that it was its source, or perhaps its primary vector for expression. Since she was consumed with him, she wanted to know all about his sadness, not out of idle or voyeuristic curiosity, but because everything about him mattered deeply to her.

After that night, she wooed him, gently, lightly, with all the restraint her years of experience allowed her. She planned very little strategy and operated chiefly on intuitive impulse. It was a matter, she thought, of working to get from P to Q and not being sure how to accomplish it. Nights, alone, she lay awake fantasizing the detailed possibilities of exactly what Q might be. Days and evenings, she spent every possible minute with Alain— sitting in on his practice sessions, watching his performances, and taking him away from his colleagues as often as possible.

The third evening they spent together— this time following an informal performance given in a cafe that was a more seriously intelligentsia venue than the Bellona Cafe— they talked, in Florentine's room, drinking wine, until four in the morning. Despite her excitement, her body began to scream for sleep long before that hour. But she didn't want to let him go, didn't want to let him leave. Through the night, Alain talked at length about his personal philosophy, his friendships, his childhood. Florentine thought she understood him. She felt close to him, as if the touch of their bodies would take her inside his skin and merge them bone to bone, soul to soul. She really, really, really wanted to fuck him. As, over the hours, they talked, sitting on the rug, drinking, they had moved closer and closer, until their knees were all but touching, their heads, constantly leaning closer, only inches apart. Her body grew wild for him. His penis, she found herself thinking, was in very easy reach. Only a touch, she thought, only a touch and everything else would follow, since nature would simply have to take its course.

Nature! That's how much *she* knew. Later she would bitterly ask herself if anything in Blue Downs could ever be *natural*, and answer: only as "natural" as the light in the Church of the One True God, where access to the sun was blighted by the cathedral looming over it.

Having decided her move, she lingered on the verge of making it, simply for the pleasure of anticipation. The possibility of being refused never entered her head. Her sole care was for sparing them the little awkwardnesses that commonly attended sexual scenes with the inexperienced, awkwardnesses that smooth orchestration by the experienced party could mute, if not eliminate altogether.

On and on Alain talked. Seriously, rather than garrulously, carefully rather than pretentiously. He was talking about how

his grandparents were musicians, particularly about his grand-
mother, Sheridan, who had been born into an affluent merchant family and been expelled when she chose to become a
composer of mixed electronic and live music rather than serve
as high priestess of the family's business and fortune. At last,
unable to wait a single moment longer, Florentine brushed
her fingers over his knee and slid them along the inside of
his coarse cloth-clad thigh. Her heart pounded, and her breath
caught in her throat as the thrill of the touch coursed through
her body. She looked into Alain's eyes, which first widened
with surprise and then frowned with perplexity as her fingers moved on to the artistic little codpiece, an item of Big
Blue fashion that was de rigueur for males of all classes and
ages. His perplexity took Florentine by surprise— at the same
moment that her fingers discovered what felt like a less than
full erection beneath the codpiece.

"Um, Florentine?" Alain said, as though to inquire what
possible reason she might have for stroking his genitals.

His response confused her. How could anyone not know
the meaning of one person— whose face and neck is flushed,
breath fast and short, fingers trembling— stroking another
person's genitals? As she watched her angel's face dance its
way through a series of swift, rapid changes of expression as
elusive as a sequence of fleeting shadows, her confusion
slipped over the border into the fascinated precincts of wonder. She saw astonishment, gratification, doubt, and pleasure
pass across his face, to be succeeded, with heartbreaking fi-
nality, by sadness and firmness of resolution. As she watched,
his face tilted slightly, bringing the light to shine in such a
way as to bounce with a glare off the suddenly glazed surface
of his eyeballs; she shivered a little, for something about that
trick of the light sent a shaft of icy wind down her bones. She
recognized the sadness, of course, for she'd been catching
glimpses of it lurking around the edges of Alain's social self
all along.

His hand settled over hers, which was searching for the Velcro seam that she presumed must be securing the codpiece's closure. "Florentine," he said tenderly, urgently, "It never crossed my mind that you didn't *know*. You comprehend so much about everything, and you're something of an expert, for a foreigner, anyway, about Blue Downs. So I just assumed you knew that. . . ." He blushed, running up against the internalized constrictions of speech that so limited open verbal acknowledgment of what was assumed to be obvious in his culture. For the first time since Florentine had met him, he looked uncomfortable and embarrassed.

There followed a strange jumble of medical jargon and awkward euphemistic evasions, but Florentine took in only the painful, basic outlines of the story he told. Alain had stood out, virtually from infancy, as a musical prodigy with an exceptionally gifted voice. Much— oh much, much, *much*— had been made of it. He learned, very early, to identify himself with his voice. He had hardly even known how to be a boy, much less a child. His father, like his mother, was a dancer. They eked out a living with difficulty. And then Magdalene had her accident, which had resulted in a broken ankle and virtually ended her days dancing. Though as a moderately successful dancer she had been a frequent soloist, she hadn't reached the stratospheric level of success and so did not command even halfway decent fees for teaching. The family's income grew marginal, its existence hand-to-mouth, with expulsion to a workfare camp for indigents just one short illness of either parent away.

When Alain began the early stages of puberty, the Blue Downs Arts Foundation approached Alain's parents and offered them a small grant and the full funding for Alain's entire musical education if they agreed to have Alain's puberty interrupted during the fourth stage, to prevent the usual changes to his vocal chords. It would be simple and painless, they were assured. The gonadostat, a regulatory center in the hypothalamus, modulates gonadotrophin secretion. Increasing serotonin and particularly melatonin levels in the blood plasma was sufficient to cause the gonadostat to decrease gonadotrophin secretion. Maintained long enough, this treatment would eventually arrest puberty— permanently.

Alain, in other words, was a new form of that archaic creature historically known as a *castrato*. Oh, he still had his testicles. His penis, larger than a child's though quite a bit smaller than a normal adult's, was capable of erections and ejaculations. But his sexuality was thwarted.

Although Florentine was shocked and indignant to learn that his parents had allowed this to be done to him— and that a respected institution of the arts had actually *promoted* it— she said at once that she didn't care if he wasn't a mature adult male sexually, that she still wanted him, still desired him, still burned for him, and that it didn't matter a jot to her what kind of sex they had, so long as he wanted, desired, and burned for her, too.

"I didn't know," he said. "Florentine, I didn't know it was possible for anyone to *desire* me— that way. Everyone said, the counselors, especially, that since I can't produce sperm, I don't have the right pheromones to attract partners. They said that would make it easier on me. To keep chaste, I mean."

"Chaste?"

Florentine didn't know the word and didn't particularly care to. Her focus at that moment was on his not answering her implicit question— whether *he* wanted *her*. Sexually. But this word, *chaste*, as she soon was forced to learn, was one of the big ones in Blue Downs. It mattered tremendously to Alain, particularly at that moment. It was a word she soon came to loathe and detest, even if she never did manage to understand its importance to her beloved.

7.

"Chaste," said Alain, his hand still over Florentine's, lying against his codpiece and the small treasure within, "means
not ever having any kind of sexual contact with anyone, including with oneself. It means being sexually pure of mind,
thought, and deed. Which not only has religious significance,
but makes one a more powerful artist."

It took Florentine the better part of a minute to think
through his explanation— which included, as part of the definition of *chaste*, the rationalization he had been given for why
he needed to apply it to himself.

"Obviously, if you believe being *chaste* makes you a more
powerful artist, this matters," she said carefully, trying not to
betray the irony she felt toward the very idea in the tone
of her voice. "I don't quite see how that would work, except by
way of a crude model of sublimating your libido. Do you also
find the religious significance— this *purity* you talk about—
important to you as well?" Religion was not something that had
arisen in any of their conversations, so naturally Florentine imagined she was posing a rhetorical question.

"It's all connected," he said. Florentine's heart sank. "I
have to admit I'm not especially *devout* in my practice— I
hardly go to church, except to perform. But. . .although I'm
lax, there's no question that it *matters* to me. I mean, my Voice
is a gift— a really special gift. Unlike other musicians, who
have nonanimate instruments they can rely on and only have
to worry about technique, *my* instrument— what makes me
the musician I am— is produced through my body— a special gift from God. It could be taken from me at any time."
Blushing, as though only now noticing that he had been pressing Florentine's hand against his penis, he pulled her hand
away from his codpiece and held it between both of his. His
eyes looked as intense as she'd yet seen them. Passionately, he
said, "It's only by God's grace that I possess such an instrument
at all. Which is something, Florentine, I never, never forget."

Florentine placed her other hand over the top one of Alain's, making a quadruple-deck sandwich of their hands. "How terrible, to have to worry about losing your voice," she said. "Is this fear typical of singers?"

The question launched Alain into a lengthy spiel about how there had never been a serious singer in the history of the species who hadn't suffered, constantly, from this fear. Why a simple cold or allergy could completely disable a singer! A cough! Anemia! Hiccoughs! A lengthy litany of health complaints poured out of Alain with such force that Florentine found herself concluding that all singers— including Alain— must harbor a fierce tendency to hypochondria.

If Alain's vehement diatribe wasn't the focus of passion she was interested in, at least it got him off the subject of religion. And it allowed her an opening from a different direction when, commiserating with him about the fragility of his gift and his dependence, as a musician, on his good health and well-being, she gently embraced him in a lingering hug of empathy, then nuzzled his cheek and softly kissed his lips— "chastely." He did not retreat in alarm. So Florentine's second kiss, deployed in a masterful stealth attack, resulted in a quivering, timid response that soon grew interesting. . . . Inevitably, though, as his excitement mounted and their caresses became bolder and more intimate, Alain pulled back, gasping, troubled, breathless, and trembling. "Oh God," he whispered. "Oh God. Now I've done it." Slowly the color drained from his passion-flushed face. He pressed his hands to his mouth as though he'd just learned he'd made the worst mistake of his life.

"What is it, darling, what is it?" Florentine's hand moved to stroke his hair, but he seized it and shoved it away.

"You can't understand," he said miserably. "I know all of this is as incomprehensible to you as Matrix Aesthetics."

She pressed him, of course, and coaxed him and gentled him until he revealed, halting and stuttering, that he'd had an orgasm. Which was something, it turned out, he'd never before experienced while awake. At first she thought he feared he'd never be able to sing again (by way of some bizarre superstition about ejaculation), but a stranger story than that emerged, and his halting embarrassment shifted to tearful anxiety. It seemed that when they'd arrested his puberty, he'd taken a "solemn vow" never to use his penis sexually. According to the terms of his vow, his voluntary violation of it— by having sexually ejaculated while awake— would entail his expulsion from Blue Downs' professional association of musicians, upon which hinged his employability as a singer.

Florentine was incredulous. She couldn't believe such a ridiculous entailment could possibly be legal, and she said so.

"You don't understand Blue Downs," Alain said sadly. "The courts would never interfere with the enforcement of such a vow. Vows are as binding as any mutual contract."

Florentine was nonplused. "Well then you must simply never *tell* anyone. *I* certainly won't."

He swallowed and looked away as the tears standing in his eyes threatened to overflow. "There's no way I can't tell. To stay in good standing in my church, even if I don't attend Sunday services regularly, I do need to attend a monthly community confession group. While nocturnal emissions aren't violations of my vow, they are sins that I have to confess, sins that remind me that castration is no safeguard of my chastity. What I'm saying is, that even such petty sins, as embarrassing and humiliating as they are to confess, always come out in group, even if I'd rather not publicly admit to them. Because people often try to hide their sins from themselves, not to mention their neighbors, we all have to take a drug that makes us volunteer the truth." He stared bitterly down at his hands. "I won't have any choice but to tell the whole sorry story."

Sorry story— how these words stung Florentine, like one of the penitentials' lashes flicking at her breast. The only thing sorry about their heretofore lovely evening, she thought, was the way these barbarians were holding her love's sexuality hostage. As though it weren't his own private business to use or not as he wished! As though it were some precious community possession more important than the wonderful music he made with his exceptionally powerful voice! As though he weren't a fully embodied human being made of flesh and bone.

"Well let me tell you something, Alain." Florentine grabbed his hands and made him look at her. "If they don't want your gift on *this* world, there's a whole galaxy out there that's just yours for the plucking. Where this chastity stuff is *irrelevant*." Listening to her own words, she suddenly caught fire. The possibilities thronged her imagination. She had no doubt that Alain had the potential for becoming a performance god. Talent, beauty, presence— what more did it take? The rest, *she* could provide! The connections, the organization, the strategizing. . . . Shit, she was *tired* of being a travel critic. She'd done that. She was jaded. She was ready for something new, something different.

Eagerly she shared her vision with Alain; magically, it swept away his blues. So they didn't want him? He'd just leave! As for sinful unchastity. . . . Well. He had already broken his vow. He had no reason to hold himself back from total, full engagement in adult, sexual love.

And the rest of the night— what little remained of it— was bliss.

8.

Though she had begun the evening under the influence of a powerful sexual infatuation, by morning Florentine discovered herself in total, overwhelming, mindfucking love. It might have been the vision she had of the trail Alain and she would together blaze across the galaxy that moved her from a traveler's indulgence in a momentary seduction to major emotional— and financial— commitment. For now she saw herself dedicating her own talents and resources to creating a brilliant career for him; she saw her life changed at a stroke.

When, finally, Alain fell into exhausted sleep and Florentine, too excited, lay for another half hour awake, she entertained the possibility that in a more civilized world, Alain could probably enjoy the effects of a completed puberty without sacrificing the fineness and wonder of his prepubescent vocal chords— *not* that the sex they'd had hadn't been everything delicious and satisfying, but because it made sense to her that he should be made whole, if possible, and that the sadness always lurking in his eyes, even when he was happiest, be made to vanish.

In that wakeful half hour, Florentine became convinced that they could have it all, provided only that she put everything she had into making it happen. If, after the long march of years, she had never given her heart to any of her many lovers, she did so now, as if she were an innocent young thing, unaware of the pain doing so necessarily risked.

Although Florentine had a schedule to follow, although Alain had a rehearsal in the morning and a gig in late after noon, they slept, entwined, well into midafternoon. Florentine woke with a feeling of pleasure, of something wonderful having happened, a feeling that she hadn't known since childhood. She lay still for a few minutes, listening to Alain's breathing, watching his face, so young and perfect, his lashes long and thick against the downy curve of his cheekbone, free of all care and concern, unaware of the power he already commanded. Just the touch of his hand, where it lay in sleep with its edge lightly brushing her hip, made Florentine feel so warm, so loving, that quietly getting up and going into the bath for a shower felt something like a rupture of her flesh.

Florentine knew well the pull of obsessive sexual passion, but this was entirely new to her. She was enchanted rather than addicted. She felt something being born rather than blotted out.

Standing under the hot, needle-point shower, she remembered how embodiment-positive she had first found Alain's voice. She knew it was right to take him away. Every creative fiber of that man knew the joy of embodiment. The bullshit about purity and chastity was ideological nonsense. It had to be a contradiction eating away at his soul. Once liberated from his awful world, he would realize that and be at peace, in the way he had not been when they'd finally called it a night.

Florentine found it impossible to think he was anything but an unwilling captive to his religion, caught up in its legalistic coils, its brainwashing methods, its terrorizing auto-surveillance system. All he needed, she believed, was freedom, and his life would open before him as he had never before imagined it could.

But the substantiality of Alain's internalization of this ideological terrorism confronted her directly on her finishing in the bathroom. Alain had woken in a state. As he rushed into his clothes, he made a point of avoiding eye-contact. And he muttered. "What have I done, what have I done? I'm ruined!" When Florentine tried to take him in her arms, he resisted almost violently. It was as though all the hours of talk had been idle fantasizing. In the light of day, he could no longer believe in even one word of it.

He no longer believed she loved him. Her assurances failed. He said he knew he was a freak, scarcely half a man. He said that she had made a fool of him— because he had been weak and foolish enough to let her.

Florentine hardly knew how to counter what seemed to her like madness. All she could think to do was to get him to wash his face and have a cup of coffee before rushing off. She made him believe she'd judge him rude if he did not.

Somehow she got him to settle down and look at her. She showed him the love in her eyes, she reminded him of the promises they had made in the hour before dawn. And then Alain reminded himself of the stark, plain fact that he had burned all his bridges and was finished as a singer if he did not leave the planet with her.

Still, he was stiff, and sore, and grieving. He might be gaining a life, but he had lost his world. Florentine felt, in her heart, that he was back to secretly thinking of their relationship as a "sorry story" rather than a grand passionate tale of love. But she was certain his heart would open to her again. Such harsh, painful ambivalence was to be expected. The stakes were so terribly high— for both of them.

9.

The next few days flew by like a golden, shimmering dream. Florentine resumed her schedule, and Alain resumed his. They spent every moment in which their schedules didn't conflict together. Alain filed an application for an offworld passport. He was told that it would take ten or so days to be processed. Florentine canceled her reservations and left her tickets open. She could not book tickets for Alain until he had been assigned a passport number.

Everything seemed to be going just fine, but on the third night, when they were out to supper after a concert Alain had done with a small chamber ensemble, he began to get that haunted look back in his eyes, the look that Florentine associated with his "sorry story" state of mind. It came, she thought, from exposure to his mother, who had sat beside Florentine during the concert and had looked disturbed when Florentine indicated that she wasn't interested in joining Magdalene and Alain's musician friends at the Cafe Bellona afterwards. Florentine had no fear that Magdalene suspected anything. (Her plan was to keep everyone in the dark until an hour or two before departure.) But Magdalene made it plain she thought it peculiar that Alain chose a private over a social evening.

"Darling," Florentine said after she'd told him how riveting his voice had been that night. "What you're doing takes an enormous degree of will and courage. I know it must be terribly difficult to think of leaving your family and friends, and frightening to leave the only world you've ever known. But you owe it to your voice, you owe it to yourself, and you owe it to your manhood to do it." She tried to pour out, through her eyes, her immense confidence in his courage. And she told him again about the city-state of Celestia, on Gray's World, the very heart of the transgalactic music industry, and reminded him of some of the artists he himself admired, who lived there.

"My manhood?" Alain said faintly, as though he had no idea what Florentine could possibly mean by the word. "I'm not really a man," he said, frowning. "I don't think—"

"Of course you're a man!" Florentine thought of his arrested puberty and his beardless face and unmanly vocal chords and suppressed the impatience his doubt provoked in her. "Whatever people have been telling you, you're not to doubt *that!*"

He did not argue the point, but something in his expression made her think he didn't agree. He said, instead, "I wonder just how much courage I have. God knows that I owe a great deal to my Voice."

They drank champagne and ate bread and paté and fruit and agreed to talk instead about the chamber group he had performed with. Alain was terribly fragile, Florentine thought. Her big bold plan could fall apart at any moment with just the right kind of push from someone wanting to thwart it. Somehow she had to get them through the days remaining without that happening. Her primary strategy must be to keep him as occupied as possible. It was Magdalene's interference, not Alain's lack of resolution, that worried her.

Quite correctly, as it turned out.

10.

Magdalene took Florentine by surprise two days later. Florentine was off guard, sipping wine on the terrace of a restaurant on the Plaza of Glory, reviewing the list of hotels prior to determining which one should receive her patronage when her contracted time ran out and she would have to start paying her own way. Some mildly pleasant, if canned, lute music played in the background. The place was new, but showed all the signs of being attractive to tourists. Since Alain had promised to join her for the midday meal, when she heard the scrape of the chair on the flagstones, she assumed his arrival. "A few seconds, darling, and I'll be done," she said, making the universal gesture indicating her engagement on-line.

"Darling," Magdalene said in a tone of disgust.

Florentine disengaged and faced a Magdalene she did not know. The usual display of deference, admiration, and the eager desire to please had been replaced with coldness and determination. She had squeezed Alain, Florentine thought, and he had told her. "I was expecting Alain," she said, imagining that a reminder of Magdalene's rudeness at joining her without an invitation would bother her.

"Alain asked me to come in his place."

"Oh really. Then shall we order?"

Magdalene's mouth twisted. "Do so, if you like. I want nothing more than water."

She appeared to be too upset to eat— a place Florentine was heading for fast, herself. But she had no intention of letting Magdalene see that. So she did order, only a far lighter meal than she had originally intended.

To put Magdalene on the defensive, Florentine said, "So if you don't intend to eat, why is it that you felt it necessary to come in Alain's place?"

Magdalene folded her hands on the table before her. Though her voice sounded cool and unstressed, her knuckles were blanched. "Alain came to see me this morning, before his rehearsal. He said he'd ruined his life. And that faced with that ruin, he had agreed to run away from Blue Downs, with you. I had no idea what he meant by *ruined*. Then he explained. It seems he thought that because he'd soiled his specialness, he'd no longer be able to perform in Blue Downs. I told him I doubted that was true. Granted, he'd forfeited his special position, but with church-guided penitence and reparation, cleansing his sin and restoring one part at least of his specialness, the Association will certainly agree to let him perform again. I've heard of such cases in the past. In Blue Downs, no one is held to be permanently beyond the pale. Our society is very forgiving to the *truly* penitent. It was only because Alain was so overwhelmed by the enormity of breaking his vow that he thought he was beyond forgiveness."

She paused to sip from her water glass, then continued in that same calm and quiet voice. "He was so upset, when he came to me, convinced he had to choose between working as a musician, using his gift, and his life and loved ones in Blue Downs. He cursed his own weakness— unable to resist ejaculating, he said, when he touched your breasts. He wept bitterly at his having allowed his sexual desire full consciousness. It was fitting, he said, that he be forced into exile as the price of continuing to use a gift he had betrayed. And I saw that my son was utterly crushed at the prospect. When I explained that such a choice would not be demanded of him, it was as though an intolerable burden had been lifted from his heart."

She paused to take several more swallows of water, and Florentine stared at the hard determination in her face. "Which was such a relief to me, since he almost instantaneously became himself again. As though nothing could ever be so terrible as the moments, hours, and days he had spent convinced he was facing exile." Magdalene lightly cleared her throat. "Of course, free of that burden, his next concern was for your feelings." Magdalene's expression was now *pitying*

"*My* feelings!" . Florentine felt outraged that this woman dared even *mention* them. She had intruded into a private relationship that was really none of her business. "My *feelings*," Florentine said sharply, "are not up for discussion in this conversation. At least not my feelings for *Alain*."

The first course arrived; carefully Florentine focused on it and the service in case she decided to use the recording she was making of it for the travelogue, or in case GTI wanted to use it in their Blue Downs restaurant guide.

Magdalene continued. "My son said you know so little about Blue Downs that he didn't think he could make you understand, himself, how important it is for him to stay. Important for his music, important for his identity, important for his *soul*."

Florentine picked up the narrow, two-tined fork, glanced briefly at Magdalene, and dug into the dish of lightly-sauced shellfish. She had a fair idea of what was going on. Magdalene had browbeaten Alain into disavowing his feelings for Florentine and now he was afraid to tell her himself, knowing, as he did, that she would not accept the triumph of his mother's will in the face of his moral weakness. Magdalene had put him in an unforgivably humiliating position. Florentine could not blame him for wanting to avoid putting that humiliation on display.

The shellfish was delicious, and Florentine was careful to give it her best recording gaze. "His *identity*?" She scoffed openly at the word. "It seems a full, mature identity is the last thing he's likely to find if he stays in Blue Downs. No thanks to the parents who have allowed him only a partial manhood totally unnecessarily." Florentine had checked a good medical source and confirmed her suspicion that it was perfectly feasible to prevent the thickening of the vocal chords without sacrificing genital maturity. "Any competent endocrinologist could have saved his prepubertal voice without arresting the full development of his virility, Magdalene." Though her throat was tight with distress, she swallowed another tender morsel, then looked directly at Magdalene. "I can't begin to understand how parents claiming to love their son would choose to mutilate him. No matter how much money they were offered to do it."

That brought some garishly hectic color into the smooth, olive-skinned cheeks. Now, Florentine thought, her coolness would dissolve into anger and outrage at the older woman of the world seducing her innocent young son. She would resort to clichés, and Florentine would find it easy to show her her shallowness for doing so.

Magdalene said, "You keep talking about manhood. Obviously you have some idea of making him into a *full, mature, adult male.* You may be a sophisticated galactic traveler, Florentine, but it's obvious you have a pretty simplistic idea about gender. What you fail to understand is that no matter what his sexual physiology might be made to be, Alain will never be a *man.* That isn't his identity. Which you apparently don't recognize, much less acknowledge. As I pointed out to Alain, it's unlikely anyone would recognize his gender anywhere off this planet. It doesn't exist elsewhere. So always he'd have to be pretending— while never feeling recognized for who he is." She nodded. "I see from your face that you have no idea what I'm talking about. You imagine that he is a man— a *partial* man— that needs only a little correction to be made *full.* You don't see Alain for what he is, under the skin."

The second course arrived, and though Florentine was distracted, she tried to do her focus on it justice. But before she took even one bite of it, she had to look at Magdalene and say, "You claim he isn't a man and never will be. But if he's not a man, what is he, Magdalene? A neuter? A drone? An *it?* Or an eternally pubescent *boy?*" Keeping her son eternally a boy would suit a woman like Magdalene just fine, Florentine thought as she picked up her soup spoon.

Magdalene took her time replying. "Florentine, you make me really, really sad. I would have thought someone so little interested in family life as yourself would be able to imagine there are other paths the human being can take than the sexual and reproductive." She leaned back in her chair. "You will scoff, but in Blue Downs we call those who do not finish puberty 'earthly angels.' They are respected and admired and envied in ways you could not begin to comprehend. The specialness of Alain's kind lies in their being exempted from the ordinary duties and concerns and messy entanglements of the body and spirit that any kind of sexual relationship entails. The *reason* most religions consider sexuality problematical is because, unregulated, it throws the individual off-balance, at the mercy of illusions, hormones, and persistent misunderstanding. Alain was to have been spared all that. Devoted to art, he would never have known such loss of self, loss of control, loss of certainty. He's fallen now. And though he'll recover, he'll never be the same. He'll always have a tendency to wonder if it would have been better had he become a man. And people will know that he violated his sacred trust and is not quite as special as he was. Which is why his act of penitence must be correspondingly severe. His submission will be proof that though altered, he is still special. A fallen angel, perhaps, but an angel nevertheless."

"An angel!" Florentine shoved the barely-tasted cup of soup away from her. "It's like a mass psychosis! You're all fucking brainwashed!"

Somehow she got through the rest of the meal while Magdalene droned on and on about Alain's "specialness." Magdalene said that Florentine was disrespectful of Blue Downs mores. Florentine pointed out that a society's mores are not always deserving of respect and demanded that Magdalene admit that she agreed with her about *that.* Surely she wouldn't respect a society that ritually ate other humans, would she?

When Florentine had finished sampling a bite or two from every course she had ordered, Magdalene insisted that she accompany her to the Plaza of Penitence. She said she wanted to show her something. Statues faced the Plaza of Penitence on three sides, Florentine knew, and so she expected to be shown one whose significance she had missed— presumably a glorification of the "specialness" of Blue Downs' "earthly angels." She agreed to Magdalene's demand because she thought it the best way to get out onto the street and positioned for a fast getaway.

In fact, Magdalene's object was a good deal uglier.

Florentine heard the sounds of a mean, nasty crowd when they were only a block from the Plaza— jeering catcalls and angry invective, scary with the visceral overtone of a mob on the verge of losing the last vestige of civilized constraint. She pulled up short and glared at Magdalene. "I'm really not in the mood to watch some unfortunate wretch who's suffered a reversal of material fortunes get beaten up by a mob prior to being tossed out into the scrublands. Public beatings are disgusting enough, but the fear and loathing of failure in your society makes such beatings positively barbaric."

Magdalene's lips pressed tightly together as her suddenly angry, narrow gaze scoured Florentine's face. Until their exchange at lunch about Blue Downs' mores, Florentine had always gone out of her way to be tactful about the uglier aspects of Blue Downs. Naturally, this unaccustomed criticism infuriated Magdalene. "An elder of the Church of Repentance and head of one of the most important merchant families in the city is making a major act of penitence in the Plaza. I want you to see at least a few minutes of it, so that you can have some small idea of how brave and determined Alain must be to submit himself to the same process. Some people do prefer to run away, to accept exile off-planet rather than commit themselves to the pain and humiliation of public repentance. You will never have even the glimmering of an understanding of what's at stake for Alain unless you see what he is willing to undertake to retain his specialness."

Florentine was sickened at the thought of what must be happening in the Plaza, but given Magdalene's argument, could not refuse her demand.

They walked the remaining block to the Plaza and joined the fringe of the violent, jeering mob. And then Florentine watched with revulsion and disgust, recording every ugly abuse she saw. It wasn't the most brutal thing she had ever watched, but the stress Magdalene laid on its voluntary performance by the victim made it, hands down, the most nauseating. The man being beaten and defiled would, Magdalene said, survive, though it would take him months to heal physically.

Florentine knew the man would never be the same and that the ordeal would surely stamp his spirit with its inhuman savagery forever.

The last thing Magdalene said to Florentine, when they parted, was that Alain intended to visit her in her suite at the B&B early that evening. *Good,* Florentine thought. *Because I'm not going to let Magdalene do all his talking for him, as though he's some scared young boy hiding behind his mother's skirts.* But the cold, metallic thought that he had already decided he would prefer to go through with such an ordeal rather than leave the planet with her pierced Florentine like a spike being driven into her heart. She no longer believed that she could counter the brainwashing that shaped and distorted his every emotion and idea. She understood that she wasn't up against just his mother, but the entire horror of a society he'd been born and raised in.

11.

Her one thought while waiting for Alain was to assert the reality of who they were together, of who he was to *her*, with her— of who they would be in the future, together. The key to this lay in their bodies, in their very embodiment, which was what in their designation of Alain's "specialness" Blue Downs sought to deny above all.

Alain, however, when he arrived at Florentine's door, would not allow her to touch him, not even to exchange the ritual double kiss. When he was safely over the threshold, she made the door close and said, "You're afraid of acknowledging what you really want."

In his lovely face— an angel's, indeed, she thought bitterly— Florentine confronted a pain so harsh that she nearly cried with vexation at its utter gratuitousness. "I'm afraid of a lot of things, Florentine. That is true." His voice was as buttery and steady as ever, but lacked its usual lilt and buoyancy. "I'm sorry for all the hurt I'm causing you," he said. "But I've come to say goodbye."

Desperation made her reckless. "Your loyalties are misplaced. Do you realize how unnecessary it was for them to deprive you of a completed puberty? You could *have* your voice *and* mature sexuality *both*! The sacrifice they demanded of you was totally artificial! And it still is!"

His eyes— reminding Florentine, so wrenchingly now, of Magdalene's— pitied her. "What lifts a species beyond the merely instinctual is the exercise of intentionality, Florentine. That's why art is the pinnacle of all that is best in human beings. It uses natural materials but is entirely, consciously artificial as it does so. That's what you still haven't grasped about Matrix Aesthetics. If anything exemplifies how Matrix Aesthetics works, it's my gift and the terms which frame my use of it." His hands swept into a graceful arc, turned palm up, and lifted slowly to the level of his eyes. "To you it's merely philosophy, isn't it."

"Religion, philosophy," she said despairingly. "It's sick to mutilate oneself for an abstraction."

He forced a strained, wry smile. "As if you and every other human in the galaxy don't do that every day of your existence in one way or another. The difference is that I'm aware of doing it, while you are not. And I'm therefore intentionally choosing." He dropped his arms to his sides, then folded them across his chest. "Think of me as being selfish in choosing for myself rather than for you, Florentine, if that will help. Out there, off-planet, I'd never fit in no matter what I did. I need the context of a world of artists practicing Matrix Aesthetics. I need an audience that understands the emotional, spiritual, and social significance of my Voice. Not people who think my Voice is 'riveting' or 'ravishing' or just plain 'pretty'. And I can't get that anywhere but in Blue Downs."

What could Florentine answer to that? Tell him he'd carve out a new niche for himself? He didn't want to be an exception— a "freak" as he had more than once worried to her he would become off-planet. In the context he had forced onto her, their love could only be a "selfish" intrusion of hers, not something equally important to both of them.

Florentine bowed her head in defeat. She had lost. Blue Downs' ideological terrorism, Blue Downs' artistic glory, had triumphed. The pleasures of the flesh posed a feeble opposition indeed. She knew when she was beaten.

12.

Florentine devoted the remainder of her stay in Blue Downs to documenting the ugly underside that usually went unnoticed and unremarked by tourists. She haunted the Plaza of Penitence, she interviewed priests and ministers and counselors about group confession and acts of penitence. She even tried to schedule a trip out to the scrubs, to get a look at the city's dumping place for the homeless (where she expected to find merely piles of bones, since the people dumped there were usually bloody and broken from their *involuntary* acts of penitence), but ran out of time before it could be arranged. Because she could not bear to see Alain again or be reminded of what they had lost, she avoided all the arts venues she had previously haunted and the neighborhood in which Alain and all his friends lived.

Images of her "earthly angel" haunted her third and final tour of Blue Downs. She would never love anyone as she loved him. She knew she could never bear to love anyone so desperately again. She told herself that perhaps some day he would tire of his "specialness," tire of his immaturity, and choose at last to step down from his perversely proud pedestal. If that day were to come, she vowed, she would be there, still, for him— waiting for her fallen angel, waiting for the man he had so far refused to allow himself to become, waiting for the perfection of deep and total love that few people in any world were ever given to know.

The Apprenticeship of Isabetta di Pietro Cavazzi

But yes, it is true, that I, Isabetta Cavazzi, daughter of Pietro, have this twenty-third day of March, in the year of our Lord 1626, been received here in the Via del Galliera, into the Casa del Soccorso di San Paolo, which some call the "Malmaritate," though most here have been dishonored rather by their lack of husbands than by the unhappiness of their unions.

(*Io, Isabetta di Pietro Cavazzi. . . .*)

Never did I imagine that I would find myself in such a place. It is like a convent, only none of us are nuns. (Though they say that sometimes women who come here do indeed become nuns.) Through Mona Gentile's benevolence, I enjoy the privilege of a private room, for which she has agreed to pay an extra sixteen lire a month. The poorest here, with the least connections, toil day and night performing the dirtiest and most arduous of chores, and sleep in a common dormitory. I must, Mona Gentile told me, be very quiet and mannerly and docile. In that way I will help achieve the end toward which we together strive.

In fact, most of the women here are prostitutes who have fallen on hard times, unable even to pay the Ufficio delle Bollette the fee for being licensed.

I write these words in secret, in accordance with the counsel given me by Mona Gentile last night when she furnished me with this little notebook. If it becomes too difficult to keep all that is in my mind and heart from passing my lips, it is better that I write it down, because concealing words written on paper is easier than stopping up the flow of a confidence once made. "Trust no one to keep unspoken anything that you tell them. You know how easily gossip flows from one to the next. And above all, neither confide nor confess anything about our affairs to any priest there you might see, since most priests lack the wisdom and sympathy of our own Don Tomaso."

(*E sopra tutto. . . .*)

Here in this place where I am subject to the rigors of the Congregation's rule and sharing a roof with those who have fallen so low, Ser Achille's laugh rings again and again in my ears. "You fool," he said to me after he struck me so hard that I fell to my knees, his voice so cruel and scornful, "Signor Alberto has given you the trick. How could you believe that such a one as you could be worthy of marrying a signore of such a magnificent family? And you," he said to Mona Gentile, shaking his finger at her as Lucia often does with Giuseppe, when he has been naughty, "how could you encourage her to imagine herself so grand? She has squandered her honor for illusions and vanity, like the poor country fool that she is. But you, my wife, knew better."

Ser Achille is wrong. My honor will be regained, and my love, too, with Mona Gentile's skillful help, God willing. Ser Achille knows nothing of the binding powers of love, or of the hammers that strengthen it where it falters (as I fear has happened with Berto). But Ser Achille knows little of his wife. And if he did, who then would be the poor country fool, eh?

Rising for chapel well before dawn is no easier than rising in the cold dark to fetch in wood and water and get the fires going. Truly, it sounded to me so easy— to lead the devout life, with my only chores a bit of spinning and needlework. But when the matron woke me from my sleep in the cold, still darkness of a night not yet finished, I could think only of the emptiness of my stomach. It growled so loudly that I could hear it even through the ugly racket of our voices singing the liturgy (without so much as an organ to help guide our pitch). Oh the chapel is a dismal one, with just the crucifix above the altar and only the one painting, of the Magdalene washing Christ's feet, which cannot be seen at all before dawn, and only poorly when the light seeps in through the one window, which is behind the altar. Kneeling, it seemed to me the cold had settled into my bones for good. I could not stop shivering. Perhaps it is best, working straightaway on rising, for then even in the bitterest cold the blood heats quickly. And breakfast seems that much nearer when you are the one preparing it yourself and when you can filch a crust of bread between trips to the well.

When Mona Gentile comes, I will tell her I need more food than they allow us. Perhaps they will give us meat when Lent is over, but though we observed Lent as Christians in Mona Gentile's house, I never felt hungry on leaving the table, as I do here. I had to bite my tongue this morning, for I wanted to insist to the matron that I should be given more because of the child. (Francesca— whom we are supposed to address as "Mona Francesca," a travesty since she has never been married— is only an old prostitute, who has been on "good behavior" for the nine months she's been here. I have already learned that she and the other two warders have their favorites. But, "Make no fuss," Mona Gentile told me.) Perhaps Mona Gentile will bring me extra food, or bribe the matron.

Many priests think fasting and hunger is good for the soul. Yet this morning in chapel I could not keep my mind on the devotions, but only thought of how much I'd like to be building the fire in Mona Gentile's kitchen, and how good it would feel to be putting a cup of broth into my stomach. Somehow this kind of hunger is different from the hunger of a fast undertaken to do the powerful things Mona Gentile has been teaching me. It is, perhaps, because then I can feel the power inside myself, being drawn upon, and fashioned, whereas going before breakfast to sing lauds seems a gesture wasted. There is holy water, and a holy candle or two, but the bareness of the chapel makes it feel as though God would never deign to set foot in the place.

Perhaps it will be different when a priest is present, saying the Mass. . .

When I took out this little book just now and looked at the pages I had already written, the ugliness of my scrawl made me think of how Ser Achille would mock it if he were to see it. In truth, I don't believe anyone but me could even read it. (Even I have trouble making out all of the words, because I have written them so closely together, with each word pressing on the last, with each line right up against the one above it.) Yet, that I can write, and read, too— and not just my name, as is the case with those of my brothers who did learn to make their names— this gives me an advantage, because it means that not only can I write down my thoughts instead of foolishly speaking them to get them out of my head, but I can also make power-writing, which is in many things better than making a hammer. . .

There are birds nesting in the roof of this house. I hear them now, flapping and billing and cooing. Doves, perhaps. Which make me think of my love, my own dear Berto, and the little bird of his that I have pleased so much. . .

(*Le columbe, forse.* . . .)

Oh yesterday was wonderful! Mona Gentile came to see me— accompanied by her sister-in-law, the Signora Consolini, whose husband is a member of the Congregation and so is held in the highest esteem in this house. Last night before sleeping— lying in sheets warm from the bricks I heated in the kitchen hearth, as the Signora Consolini insisted on my behalf that I be allowed to do— I went over and over in my mind all that had passed between us, enjoying the repetition with almost as much exaltation as I felt during her visit. She walked with her sister through the entire house before drawing me aside, asking that I show her my room. And though I had vowed to myself never to complain to her of my place here, the first thing I said when we were alone was how, if it was on account of my pregnancy that I was here, I wish I had chosen rather to abort it than to tell Berto of it and demand he restore my honor.

"Foolish child!" she said. And she remonstrated with me and said that in the eyes of all my value had risen with my pregnancy, and that if I safely delivered a healthy child it would be proof of my fertility, and that the fact that I was pregnant made the suitor Ser Achille had selected for me more eager than before to wed me, once I have had my honor repaired by staying here and living piously and chastely under the Congregation's supervision. This she said here, in this room, which is where she gave me a store of sugared almonds. (She and the Signora Consolini brought also a barrel of salted fish, which I and the others who are pregnant are to be given every morning in addition to gruel.)

And then, it being mild and midday, we went out into the courtyard and walked to and fro in the sun, our arms linked as if we were indeed mother and daughter. (And truly Mona Gentile always set herself to teach me the things mothers teach their daughters, since I left my own mother at such a tender age. And besides, that time Ser Achille exploded in wrath when it seemed to him that Berto had given me the trick, he said that this stained his own honor, because my having served in his house from the time I was eleven years put him in the place of a father to me, for that he had made a contract with my father that he would provide me with a dowry and an honorable marriage.)

"Tell me," Mona Gentile said as we walked, "do you remember the first time we talked about the special powers of the body?" And of course I remembered, so clearly, the beginning of my secret apprenticeship with her, when she began by asking me if I knew any spells, and if I had ever employed them. At which I told her of how when I was seven, and the caterpillars infested the cabbages, my mother had put the yoke on her shoulders and had me ride on it, as she walked through the fields, calling out to the caterpillars a spell she said she had called out for her mother, as her mother had before her. And that the spell was in words brought from the land her great-grandmother had lived in, *Fui, fui ruie et il mio con ti mangiuie*, which means "Flee, flee, furry caterpillars, or my cunt will eat you." The words were strange to my ears, and felt strange in my mouth, but I have never forgotten them. And after I told Mona Gentile of this spell that I knew and had made, riding on the yoke, she asked me if I understood that the power of the spell came from my being a woman— or going to be a woman. And she asked me if my mother had said why a young girl, and not herself, must make the spell. And I remembered, then, my mother saying the spell did not work if it wasn't made by a girl before she had begun issuing her flowers.

So I remembered all this yesterday when Mona Gentile asked, and when I said yes, I did remember, she then stopped and laid her hand over my womb, which isn't very big yet, and said that all the power that is mine as a woman is working now to make a human being, and she touched my breasts and said that the power was working in my breasts now, too. (I felt foolish at Mona Gentile's mention of my breasts. It was when I went to her, saying that I thought I needed the spell for *madrazza*, that she discovered I was pregnant, which I hadn't known. "And how," she said then, "would a woman who has never given birth, come to suffer *madrazza*, which is caused by an excess of milk?") "And so it is true," I asked her, "what they say about breast milk, that it is flowers stored up and cooked in the breasts?" And she said yes, which was why husbands who could afford to pay a wet-nurse would not allow their wives to suckle. (Besides, of course, their not wishing to abstain from the pleasures of the marital bed for all that time.)

In the countryside we are poor, and all women suckle. But then the rich women in the city always do send their babies away from the moment of their birth, or bring women in from the country to do that work.

My hand is too cramped to write more. And the light is getting thinner. And we will soon be called to supper, and then compline, anyway.

I woke early this morning, well before they summoned us to lauds, in the cold, still darkness. Though I had great need to relieve myself, I lingered in bed, where some of my body's warmth, at least, remained. And yet the cold did not seem that terrible to me, because I felt a great warmth kindled in my heart as I remembered Mona Gentile's visit, still fresh in my thoughts. "And why," Mona Gentile had said to me when I told her how I loathed rising for lauds, "do you think nuns and monks are obliged to do this? While it is true that all the Signori wish masses to be said for the souls of all their dead fathers and brothers and grandfathers, you may believe me that they all rest easier knowing that thousands of nuns and monks rise in the night to say matins and lauds, during the hours in which all the powers of heaven and earth are nearly extinguished, particularly in the two hours before dawn, when the earth has lost its heat, and finally even the birds become alarmed and cry frantically and pathetically their most doleful plaints, a time when even demons and spirits and angels flee the utter coldness and stillness of a dying world. And then the nuns and monks rise for lauds, seeking to touch the heart of God, lest he not let heat and life and vitality return to the earth, and lo, as the end of lauds comes, the sun rises, and life has been saved, again, from the risk of endless night. And then there is power enough to say Mass, and all living things whether incarnate or only spiritual revive, in the daily resurrection of what we call the 'new day'. . ."

Mona Gentile is so wise, understands so much! And yet is so beautiful, her eyes the most radiant blue, her hair a fiery gold that compares with the sun itself. . . It almost seems a scandal for a miserable prostitute like that little Anna Laura Spighi to whisper in my ear, "Your lady is so very beautiful," and yet it is true, and it makes the others here look at me differently, to see that such a beautiful and respectable lady as Mona Gentile takes so great an interest in me.

(*È tanta bellissima, tua donna. . . .*)

Of course I do not tell anyone here how Mona Gentile came to bestow her trust and affection on me. After all, when I first came to Ser Achille's house, I was just another miserable girl from the country hired to do the drudgery that must be done in every household, even those in the city. And I was laughably ignorant and required much scolding before I learned how to give good service. Mona Gentile had scant patience with me and seemed beyond pleasing. And my weeping with homesickness increased her displeasure. But one day she caught sight of the caule my mother had placed around my neck. ("Never, never, never part yourself from it," my mother told me. "It is what makes you special, it holds all the power of my womb when it was making you.") I was frightened, for I thought, being a fine city lady, she might make me throw it in the fire (which is what, my mother says, some priests make people do when they discover them wearing their caules, because the priests know the caules hold power and can't abide anyone else having power besides themselves). But in fact Mona Gentile spoke gently to me, and called me "sister," because she said she too had been born with a caule, and wore it next to her skin, though she never let anyone see it, especially not any man. And from then on she began to instruct me in the ways of magic, and the powers of the body and hearth. And I became then not just her servant, but her pupil, and her "sister of the caule."

But I have yet to write down (as if I could forget anything that Mona Gentile has said to me!) the rest of our conversation. It concerned Berto, and my pregnancy, and Ser Achille's plans for my future. Mona Gentile says that Berto is very pleased that I am pregnant. (And yet he will not keep his word to me! Which I do not understand!) He is concerned, she said, that I look on only beautiful things, and that I eat well, so that the child will be born healthy. (To this end, he has pledged to make a donation to this house.) If it is a boy, he will give it to a wet-nurse he will hire, and when it is weaned raise it in his house. If it is a girl— I had to prompt Mona Gentile to tell me— he will have the child taken to the foundling home. Alas, poor thing! And how many survive to live after having been taken to that place? I have heard, I had no need to ask Mona Gentile about it, because it is so well known and talked of in the city, how foundling homes were first established to take the infants of slaves, because their milk was wanted by their masters for renting out, and would dry up if they were to watch their own children die before their eyes, or else would be given them illicitly, as a theft from their masters. While there are few if any slaves in the city now, yet there are still children born for whom there is no milk, their own mothers' milk being needed for other children.

It is bitter indeed. For whether I give birth to a boy or a girl, Ser Achille will arrange a contract for me to go as *balia* to a good family in the city, for wages that will enlarge my dowry greatly (particularly since some of the portion coming to me— as well as the sheets I had sewn and laid aside— will be spent on my maintenance here). And when the child I am contracted to nurse has been weaned, I will return here briefly, and then marry.

Wet-nursing is an honorable profession, Mona Gentile said to me. But I was so upset that Berto is eager for the child, yet still refuses to publicly acknowledge me as his wife, that I said again that I wished I had taken the sage-leaf medicine, for then I would still be Berto's wife, and that besides, I would probably die in childbed. But Mona Gentile promised me she would deliver me herself and asked me did I not have faith in her powers? And of course it is true, if Mona Gentile is with me, I must be delivered safely. As for Berto, she did not need to remind me that Ser Achille owes much to Berto's father, who is the magistrate for whom Ser Achille has been a notary for many years. These city ways! I always believed in my heart that if Berto broke his word to me, that he would be made to keep it, as when I was eight years I witnessed my uncles, the priest, and the mayor besides make another who would break his word to his pledged wife, marry her as he had promised.

But "Do not despair," Mona Gentile said to me. "Pretend to agree to any arrangements Ser Achille makes for you. There is time, and opportunity, for making Signor Alberto change his mind. Do not forget the power of the hammer, my child. I promise you, Signor Alberto will be struck. We will make him come back to you, begging you to marry him. Trust me."

(*Mi credi.*)

I do, Mona Gentile, I do trust you. But how to make a hammer in a place like this? Teach me, my lady, teach me how. And if it hurts Berto— though of course not mortally. . . if it causes him pain. . .let him think then how he has caused me pain.

Yesterday when Mona Gentile visited she brought me lemon verbena, mint, and camomile, for steeping in hot water and drinking with honey (which she also brought me), the lemon verbena in the morning, the mint in the afternoon, and the camomile in the evening, before compline. Though I keep these herbs and the honey in my room, I still need to use the kitchen hearth, for getting the water. But that is part of the point! Not only are these drinks good for pregnant women, but I need access to the kitchen hearth if I am to make the hammer that will bring Berto back to me. As Mona Gentile observed yesterday, though she can prepare some of it, and place it for me, there are certain things that I must do myself. For all that my powers are diminished, because they are needed for the growing of the child, they are not entirely lost.

And so I made an appearance in the kitchen yesterday evening, not just to fetch the bricks that I heat there, but to steep the camomile leaves in hot water. Mona Elissa was there, of course. (She has a bed in the alcove to the side of the hearth, where it is nearly always warm, just as I do in Mona Gentile's house. That arrangement, plus the fact that it is she whom the Congregation entrusts with the key to the cellar, where all the food staples and wine are kept, makes her behave as if she is lady of the house. Of course it is true that she is a widow, and more respectable than any of us here, since it is only because her children are dead and her husband misused her dowry that she is in this place, which she prefers to a convent.) Mona Elissa stood with her hands on her hips, like a great black crow shrilling warnings at me, only instead of cawing, she held her lips pressed tightly together, as though to let me know that it was only because I am the Signora Consolini's protégée that she would allow me the use of her hearth.

"Accustom all who work in the kitchen to seeing you there often," Mona Gentile said. I know, without doubt, what enrages Mona Elissa. It is not that I am Signora Consolini's protégée, which is the reason the matron hates me, since she owes her position to the Signora's rival, Donna Masserenti, also the wife of a member of the Congregation. No, Mona Elissa dislikes anyone she cannot order about as a servant; and those who enter the kitchen are mostly the residents who are obliged to work for their maintenance. And so it vexes her that she lacks authority over me. She is foolish, though, for thinking herself above the factional rivalry. Coming from a mere village, I know that it is always necessary to choose sides. Even in the great city of Bologna, it is necessary. And here in this small house, it is even more necessary. Mona Elissa has not been here above two years. That is not long enough to judge the situation.

This is how foolish Mona Elissa is: "She is the Signora Consolini's little pet," that one hissed at the miserable little Catarina, who was scrubbing the enormous kettle that had been used to make the soup we ate at supper. And did she notice, that the little Catarina sent me a friendly, respectful look, as if to say that though she is a partisan of the matron, she might change sides if it were expedient?

Mona Elissa's voice is the loudest at lauds and compline, and the ugliest, too. It is a sort of nasal drone, that takes no pleasure in its own use. It's no wonder she snapped at me for humming while I waited for the little kettle Mona Gentile brought me to boil!

I woke this morning in tears, brimming with a grief I have carried with me all day. I dreamed a thing unbearable, I dreamed the one thing I haven't allowed myself to think might be really true, however carelessly my Berto may have behaved (and thus unthinkingly brought me to this place). I dreamed that Berto betrayed me as Ser Achille has tried to make me believe, that he deliberately gave me the trick, all the while laughing at me behind my back. In the dream it was the night of carnival in which I did that so daring thing— emboldened, perhaps, by the assurance Berto's love had brought me— that is, dressing in Rico's clothes (which because they were so large on me exposed no more than my legs, which many have seen anyway in the ordinary course of accidents life holds for girls like me). In the dream, as happened that night, Berto was amused and applauded my boldness— until Francesca appeared, and said loudly, for Berto, Rico, and all of our friends who were making beautiful dances with us: "That one will end up at the baths, she looks like one of us already." And hearing that, from one who for several years worked at the baths (and according to the portress dressed often in male clothing, and even allowed herself to be used for every kind of sodomy, including the kind that is done by men to boys), the other girls there spoke disapprovingly to me (as they did that night of the carnival), and Rico and Berto sneered, and Berto said for all to hear: "Yes, she will do well at the baths, for I have given her the trick, as she must very well know!"

Mona Gentile says that dreams are not always what they seem at first sight. But the heaviness in my heart is so sorrowful that if I dared I would have spent the day in my room, weeping. Only the thought of Francesca coming in here, playing the matron over me, taunting me for my foolishness, made me go through the motions of all that is expected of me here.

"Fear is the first great enemy of love," Mona Gentile once said to me, when she explained to me why we must never let those we are binding to us with the magical arts know of our labors for them. "Fear," Mona Gentile said, "and coldness. Hot anger is always better for love than cold. Cold anger will kill love more surely than anything else. Cold anger makes contempt." Surely I must not let fear poison my love for Berto, for that love is greater than anything I can think of, greater than my life itself. I must think of his eyes, and his hands, and his mouth, which have been so tender with me, and are unto themselves grace incarnate. I must try to remember his delight on that night of carnival when I wore boy's clothing, I must try to remember the fierce joy of our dancing, and how everyone remarked about it how perfectly we are matched. That was the reality, the dream is false, a warning against despair— and against the evil machinations of the matron.

My fear is that locked up here, I will be forgotten by Berto. Men forget the things of the body so quickly— I have heard Mona Gentile remark on this again and again. But they are written on our bodies, so that we never forget any of it, neither the pain nor the pleasure, neither the sorrow nor the joy. Which is the reason, Mona Gentile says, that magical arts are needed to bind men.

As for the question of "giving me the trick," what matters is how Berto feels about me, not that I have given him my honor, and am now without any at all. "Honor is determined by men, who manage everything to do with its arrangements," Mona Gentile said when we first talked about this. "Women are powerless in such matters, except when defaming one of their own number, since men will believe the evil one woman speaks of another, but dismiss the good; and so questions of honor do not concern us. We have other ways of making arrangements, ways in which men are in turn powerless. Let Ser Achille and Signor Alberto worry about honor; we, my child, will arrange things in our own way, and when we have done, they will make their arrangements to suit ours."

As with love, the magical arts require confidence without arrogance, in order to work. And yet, I am in despair.

Blessed Madonna, help me!

How clever of me, is it not, that I've invented my own abbreviations, to make writing so much easier! Because my fingers grow cramped so quickly, I have been reluctant to bother with writing, especially now that I seem to want to sleep all the time. But because some of us now sit outside, in the courtyard, the weather being so pleasant, with our spindles and flax, and because of the great scandal, the very details of which are yet held secret from us here, I find my tongue making too free with its desire for speaking the many things in my mind. And so, remembering how Ser Achille and other notaries use abbreviations when they write (because many times they are required to write down, at great speed, everything that is said, particularly in criminal cases, and also because many of the same expressions and phrases are used repeatedly in legal documents, and are less tedious to the hand when noted by a single mark or letter with a mark distinguishing it), it seemed to me a clever thing to invent my own set of marks. (And I note, too, that it is not a bad thing that only I know what they signify!)

The scandal— ah, that is an enigma. Three of us were out in the courtyard this afternoon, working our spindles diligently and singing pretty little ditties with only the most innocent of words, since we are forbidden to sing "love songs." (We are also forbidden to "chatter and gossip," which is why we choose to sing, since it is obvious when our voices are lifted in song that we are obeying the rules of the Congregation.) Suddenly the little Catarina came rushing out to us, sputtering with so much excitement that at first she could not get the words out. "It is impossible!" she said. "But it is true! I cannot believe it, but the Signora Messina Vignola, whom we all know, because she is the wife of Signor Flaminio Segnelli, and has often come here with other ladies, has been brought here to live! I was in the hall, scrubbing the tiles, when Mona Antonia gave entry to her and several signori, one of them the dottore, her husband!"

All of us in the courtyard believed that Catarina had misunderstood. The Signora Vignola has been here several times since I arrived. Not only does she come often with other ladies, bringing provisions and inspecting and questioning us as is usual with many of the wives of Congregation members, but it is not long since she attended the service held in our chapel on Holy Saturday, and attended the Easter feast with her husband and other Congregation members and their wives, that was given for us here in this house. But Catarina was not mistaken! It seems that the Signor Segnelli has, with the approval of other Congregation members, chosen to confine his wife here, with us! I do not understand it. For a Signor to send his own wife, a fine lady, to such a place. . .it is, as I say, a great enigma. Francesca, however, tells us we are not to speak about it, that it is none of our affair.

The lady will, of course, keep to herself. We are to treat her with the great respect we always pay the wives of Congregation members. . .

I have often heard Ser Achille, joking with Mona Gentile, call the Florentines "wise" for keeping their wives always locked up at home, with their only freedom that of peering out the smallest slits of windows, or occasionally standing on their loggias, to witness holy processions. (In that place, men as old as Ser Achille need not worry when they take wives as young as Mona Gentile!) But of course, as Mona Gentile says, everyone knows that all business and even political affairs would be thrown into confusion here in Bologna if the women were locked up. And besides, she says, a woman locked up is a prisoner, and as such an enemy to her keeper. "But Florentine women are silent as mutes," Ser Achille always retorts. "What bliss that must be, to escape the constant natterings of women!"

Many are the women who have come to this place to flee abusive husbands. (It is for that that it came to be called the "Malmaritate.") If it hadn't been that Signor Segnelli accompanied Signora Vignola here, it would be easier to believe she had fled for safety, than that he was locking her up for punishment.

I have such fine news to tell Mona Gentile, that I am more eager than ever she visit me again soon. Today, for the first time, I saw the Devil's eyes behind the flames in the kitchen hearth. I have been following, with the greatest care and diligence, her instructions that I feed a little pinch of salt to the fire daily, when Mona Elissa's back is turned, so that the Devil will consider that hearth a good place to lurk. But to tell the truth, it frightens me a little to be coaxing the Devil here, on

my own, without Mona Gentile's strength to guide and protect me. If I am to be successful in making the hammer that
will re-bind Berto to me, I must, Mona Gentile says, have
recourse not only to the powers of the saints and the holy
things of the Church, but also to a very little of the power of
hell, as well. The hammer I will make will be like the one
Mona Gentile made three years ago, to bind Signor Paolo
Suffrageneo's passions the more closely to her lest her pregnancy cause him to recoil. Of course I will not be able to walk
through the streets along the path they lead criminals to their
execution, nor afterwards walk with my hands tied behind
my back through the house, with all the doors and windows
open, speaking the Our Father for the meanest souls that have
been executed, thirty-three times. But there are other things
that will serve to make my hammer strong, and Mona Gentile tells me she has a piece of hangman's rope and some blood
that dropped from the arm of a thief when his hand was being severed.

It is not dangerous, Mona Gentile says, to have limited
contact with the Devil. We acknowledge him, so that he can
be made to work for us whenever we wish. The little bit of
salt we give him in the fire is as nothing, like the merest drop
of water in the sea. It encourages him to think that if he
helps us he might eventually snare us, as sometimes happens
with the most foolish or unhappy of women. And to treat the
Devil so is not a sin, for God could not possibly be offended
by our making use of the Devil without giving him anything
but trifles in return. Mona Gentile has discussed these things
with Don Tomaso, who told her only to be careful when having any dealings with the Devil, and to do no harm to others,
including not forcing them truly against their will.

I cannot believe my hammer could harm Berto. It might
cause him pain, for as long as it takes him to remember me
and his promises to me (which he surely did mean at the time
he made them), but I do not believe it truly against his will,

in that his will in the first place intended to do all the right things by me, and not hurt or betray me (which giving me the trick would indeed do). Are hammers necessarily implements of harm?

Certainly not!

(*Certo che non*!)

It is a question of aligning the sympathetic forces of nature to the ends to which they are meant to go. Berto was drawn to me from the beginning, as was I to him, in the most natural way possible. I could feel the power of Fortune in the warmth of that first moment, even before his beautiful smile penetrated his face, when his eyes recognized me. My face, neck, and belly suffused with a fiery blush, and such was my condition that I almost forgot that I was to give him the wine I had poured out for him and Ser Achille.

I knew, yes I *knew* in that moment. And though our passion has always been fierce, let no one deny that we knew we were meant for one another, body and soul, from the start. It was this, and not mere lust, that made me tremble through the night, sleepless, my mind burning with the memory of eyes I knew, of eyes that knew me. . .

Today, it being Sunday, we went to Mass in the chapel. A certain Don Alessandro, of whom it is said he is from Venice, preached a sermon about how the lust of women threatens the souls of both women and men, and continuously makes chaos and unleashes havoc on the good order of society. And because he talked about how women give themselves to the Devil because of their lust, I at first thought he knew that I had been throwing salt to the Devil in the kitchen hearth, and was warning me against doing any business with the Devil at all. But as it happened he spoke of witches only a little and instead, almost all of the rest of his sermon, spoke about how women who do not strive to control their terrible lust willfully and scandalously destroy their own homes and the honor of their families. And everyone sitting in the chapel knew then that the priest meant his remarks to be taken to heart by the Signora Messina Vignola. And because the Signora has brought so much trouble and acrimony into this house, making demands on every woman living here, whom she treats as her servants, and complaining constantly, which makes an assault on my ears especially, her room being next to mine, many were the smiles only barely hidden from the priest and Congregation's scrutiny.

The Signor Dottore Flaminio Segnelli, the lady's husband, was not among the Congregation members present today at Mass. (But who would choose our chapel for attending Mass, if they had a free say?)

But of course, as became clear to me later, when I heard the matron joking with the portress, whores do not put much store by *female* lust, since it is the lust of *males* that benefits their pocketbooks, and *female* lust, as they believe, though attractive to men when it is simulated, often drives men who are not already lustful away.

And this day Mona Gentile came here, to attend the Signora Messina! Since we had heard that the Congregation had ruled when it permitted the Signora Messina to stay here that it would be forbidden the wives of the members to hold any conversation with her whatsoever, this was surprising indeed! But the president of the Congregation made a special dispensation for the visit, because Mona Gentile is a healer of women's diseases. To my great joy and gratification, Mona Gentile requested that I assist her, and then she sent away the little Catarina, who has attached herself to the Signora as mud does to the feet, ankles, and fingernails of any who work in the fields.

The Signora Messina suffers from the whites— which is a thick white discharge issuing from her womb, like a continual flow of white flowers. It stains her linen, which has constantly to be changed and washed. The smell, when her skirts are lifted, is strong, not only of the odor that habitually issues from that place, but of something like the stink of hops fermenting. Mona Gentile has made a pessary for her; and because it must be changed often, it means that Mona Gentile will be visiting often, too.

It is good fortune for me— though not for Signora Messina— that her husband has made her to be locked up here. It is an ill wind that blows no good, my father was always saying to my mother.

After Mona Gentile finished attending the Signora, we came into my room— bringing the basin with the water she had used to wash the Signora Messina's privates. The basin was the one Mona Gentile often uses for far-seeing, especially when its water has been penetrated with vital, potent fluids. Mona Gentile stood in the patch of sunlight streaming in through the unshuttered window, holding this basin. After she had me compose myself, she bade me sign myself with the cross, to draw God's power into me, and then instructed me to look at the surface of the water only. And there was a shine on the water, which I knew would hold the images I wanted to see, but at first I had trouble concentrating on it only, for I kept seeing traces of the ropy white curds that had been left in the water. But after a little while it was as though the dazzle of the sun had showered gold into my eyes, for the shining surface suddenly rose up, like a liquid, radiant cloud, in the image of Berto! "My love!" I cried out. And Berto's eyes turned to me, as though he could hear me calling him, then dimmed suddenly and unaccountably. My throat closed when Berto turned his head away, as though he could not bear to see me, and the image vanished, and though my eyes were still a little blinded, when I blinked several times I saw just the basin, half-full of water in which drifted nasty bits of debris.

Mona Gentile assured me that my power to hold the image will grow stronger each time I summon it. I remembered, then, to tell her that I had felt the baby moving in my womb. She expressed joy, and said that she would tell Berto, because she knew it would please him.

When Mona Gentile came today to refresh the Signora Messina's pessary, she whispered to me that the lady's husband had been able to persuade the Congregation to keep her here only by promising them an enormous sum of money. She says that the Signora Consolini says that very few members of the Congregation know the reason Signor Segnelli wishes her to be kept here, and that those who know are telling no one, not even their own wives. When I remarked on how much quieter the Signora has become since Mona Gentile began ministering to her, how she no longer screams and screeches the whole day long, how she has even begun to treat Catarina as her special pet, rather than her slave, Mona Gentile said that the whites often turn even the most pleasant of women into raving shrews, for they cause great burning and itching in the private places, and also deprive the sufferer of sleep. The remedy in the pessaries is working, and the whites are lessening more each day. And also, Mona Gentile has been providing the lady with sleeping draughts. Lack of sleep alone makes people irritable and easily vexed, even when they lack the Signora's other afflictions.

And then Mona Gentile took the opportunity to praise the Signora's persistence and resolve. "We don't know what her husband, the fine dottore, who is good only for casting horoscopes and spouting Latin, which do nothing for afflictions like the whites, wishes to accomplish by keeping her here.

But by making war against her, he has miscalculated. Men say always, with the utmost confidence, that women lack *virtù*. But whatever drives that lady, she has more *virtù* and *forza* in her than the most relentless condottiere. She is recovering and consolidating her strength now, the Signora. Observe, my Isabetta, that she does not weep, nor pity herself. For that reason, she will prevail." As Mona Gentile spoke thus, her eyes shone, with that blue fire that makes me feel her words deep inside, where they kindle a blaze within me, that makes me more determined than ever to please her.

"The dottore has never attended a childbed," Mona Gentile said, scoffing. "Or he would know that the women who successfully bring children into the world require as great strength, determination, and fortitude, as any knight battling a thousand Turks."

And when Mona Gentile had gone, and I was down again in the courtyard spinning, I went over and over her words, and knew she meant me to take them deep into my heart. And though I had to get up often to visit the privy under the stairs, which is one of the afflictions of pregnancy, my heart sang a proud, fierce song. I, too, will prevail!

This morning the matron discovered me feeding the birds a little of the grain Mona Gentile brings me for that purpose. It was at that very moment, when the birds were descending to me with their great clatter and clack of wings, when I was throwing out the first handful from the knotted bit of cloth in which I keep it, that she screeched at me, "What are you doing, are you crazy?" And she confronted me, as though I were a great malefactor. It was bad enough, she said, that the birds lived in the eaves, and that we had to hear them night and day, cooing and crying and scrabbling about on the roof. It was bad enough that they bothered us from time to time in the courtyard, and made a nuisance of themselves in the kitchen garden. But that I encouraged them to it! That was a sin, and wasting grain that could be used for food, of which we never can get enough in this house!

In my startlement (and if truth be given, with intention), I dropped the cloth so that the grain spilled out all around me, and the birds feasted royally.

After several minutes of scolding, in which I pleaded that even the blessed holy Francis had fed the birds from his own begging bowl, the matron thought to demand of me where I had gotten the grain. Surely, she said, I must have stolen it from the pantry, and how had I done that, when Mona Elissa and the president of the Congregation are the only ones with keys to that place?

If she had asked me that question first, instead of scolding at such length, I would probably not have been quick enough to answer as I did. "Mona Francesca," I said respectfully, "I got the grain from here." And I showed her the paving stone lying loose and out of place, beneath which I usually keep my cache.

"And how did it get there?"

I did not answer, only shrugged.

She looked shrewdly at me, and then said that it would serve me right if she made me dig up all the paving stones, in case there was more grain put away there.

I am certain she will not search my room. And since she can't know why I feed the birds, she cannot threaten to have the Congregation throw me out for it. If the Signora Consolini were not providing so generously for our table, I believe she would have cut my portions, in retaliation, for the imagined theft. "Sometimes saints can be fools, and as wrong as any other sinner!" she said in the rage of the moment. Imagine, a fallen whore passing judgment on such an honored, holy saint!

Somehow, though that old biddy will be watching me with the greatest vigilance, I must find a way to keep feeding the birds. It is not enough that they live in the eaves. They must be trustful of me, and come to my hand when I tempt them. Just as I must keep feeding the fire with salt, to keep the Devil tamely by me, for when I need him. It is not enough, as Mona Gentile says, to wear the caule. One must make one's preparations, thoroughly, carefully, and with the best order possible.

It being the first new moon since the Midsummer Day, Mona Gentile brought me the wax doll and other items needed to begin preparing the hammer. Most important of these are the hairs she acquired from Berto, and a shirt of his with his blood on it, and a few strands from a hangman's rope. She said that she arranged for Berto to have a nosebleed while visiting Ser Achille, one so heavy that he soiled his shirt, and could thus be persuaded to part with it. It would have been fine enough to get the shirt, but the blood on it will of course make the hammer that much more powerful. Also, Mona Gentile managed to get a doll with a male member, which is not always possible, since one cannot then claim to be buying the doll to make into an image of a saint, or even Christ.

Oh, such a beautiful shirt, of such fine cotton! I savored the pleasure of burying my head in the cloth still redolent of Berto's scent, which conjured up memories of pleasure and delight, making it difficult for me to tear strips from the shirt, as I needed to do.

And yet, I recalled to myself very clearly and carefully how Mona Gentile prepared the hammer to bind Signor Paolo and then did everything as she had done, first pounding the paste of blood not yet whitened that I took from my left breast, holy oil, rosemary, dove feather, and the coals I took from the fire that burned in the hearth on Good Friday, then slathering half of it over the doll, around which I wrapped first Berto's hairs, some strands of the hangman's rope, and a few of my own pubic hairs, and around all that bloodstained pieces of the shirt, then piercing pins into the doll, both to secure the shirt and to bind the powers. And all the while I repeated the chant Mona Gentile had taught me, using Berto's name instead of Signor Paolo Suffrageneo's. And then I made a dough with the rest of the hairs and the paste, and wrapped the shirt around it, in reserve.

And now as I sleep with this doll each night while the moon grows to its fullness, as I stroke and speak to and instruct this doll, more and more of Berto's spirit will be drawn to it, and my own power over it will grow proportionately. I like lying with it between my breasts. It is as though it draws the swollen tenderness out, into itself. Perhaps it even draws some of the power from the milk that is cooking in them. And I like pressing the remains of that beautiful shirt against my cheek, so that I may breathe in Berto's essence, all the night long.

I will ask Mona Gentile when I next see her. If she thinks it will draw power from the child, I will not sleep with my little bird there. Flutter and clatter and clack, little bird. You are indeed mine now!

As the moon grows big, I am becoming most attached to my little toy. I feel less lonely, lying with it pressed tight against my breast. But by the holy tears of Jesus, I know it is no substitute for the real thing. It is an instrument, which contains some of Berto, as much of Berto as I can make it hold. It cannot steal my strength, Mona Gentile says, but rather it adds to it. The doll attracts power, and because the doll is mine in creation and possession, the power accrues to me, not to itself, since it is not, properly speaking, an independent entity. If it is stealing power from anyone, that is Berto.

Still, though the doll comforts me, I woke this morning very early, long before lauds, with a terrible fear stalking me, tightening my belly with cramps so overpowering that I feared the birth was coming too early. I remembered my mother speaking to a neighbor, just before my father brought me to the city. She said that "he"— meaning, I think, my father— had decided it was time that Lucia be weaned. And my mother complained that it was too soon, that the baby had only just begun to walk, and that she still could not chew very well. "He wants to get at me again, and then there will be that to go through, yet again, and God alone knows whether I'll live through it." And then the women talked about all those they knew who had died in childbed.

Ser Achille's first two wives both died in childbed. But I am not to think of this at all. When Mona Gentile brought me the doll she said that Berto asked after my health. Now is no time for doubt and despair!

What a timid creature I am, to be sure! Last night, because the moon was full, I had to take my courage in my hands and finish making the hammer. Mona Gentile gave me a draught to put in Mona Elissa's wine. Thank the Blessed Mary, it worked! Even so, I could hardly breathe for the trepidation causing my legs to tremble and my breath to strangle in my throat. It is one thing to do magic in Mona Gentile's kitchen, under her direction and auspices, and quite another to do it alone, in a place where I am forbidden by authority to be.

Earlier in the evening, before compline, while it was still light, I went out to the courtyard and softly whistled the birds to me. I was frightened of doing this because some of the shutters facing the courtyard were open. Still, I reminded myself of my determination and did what I needed to do. I chose the bird that looked to me as though it had the bravest, most Berto-like heart, and coaxed it to me with grain, and then imprisoned it in my hands. How frightened it was! More so than I (and for better reason, too). It tried, naturally, to escape, and even pecked my fingers before I managed to close the remainder of Berto's shirt around it. "Little bird," I crooned to it as I carried it to my room, held closely, under my skirts, to my swelling belly.

"Dear little bird, be mine."

(*Caro ucellino. . . .*)

I waited until the house fell into the depths of sleep. Before I did anything, I made sure that Mona Elissa lay sleeping soundly. (Talk about snoring! It is worse even than her singing, which is already the harshest, most grating sound imaginable.) In the kitchen the coals were still warm enough for me to use the new pot Mona Gentile had purchased "in the name of the Devil" for melting the holy candle bought "for Isabetta's love of Signor Alberto." Though the coals had been banked, I kept fearing that the Devil himself might appear, though I had not called him. I think I feared that more than that Mona Elissa would awaken and find me at work. While the wax melted, I removed the heart of the bird, spread it with the dough I had already used on the doll, twined a number of my own pubic hairs around it, then poured the wax over it, to seal it. All the while I chanted the spell Mona Gentile had taught me. And when it was finished, I carried the doll and the heart, now wrapped in the remains of the bloodstained shirt, to my room, and kneeling at my prie-dieu, prayed to the Madonna di San Luca that Berto's love be strong enough to make him keep his promise to me.

Mona Gentile took the doll away today. She will place it under the high altar of San Petronio, so that thirty-three masses will be said over it. After that she will give it to Angelica, a servant employed by Berto's father, whom Mona Gentile has bribed. She will secure it within Berto's bed, where it will be most potent.

Holy Madonna, grant me success!

I am overflowing with a great beauty— which I, having
taken into my heart and mind, now take part in its radiance!
And this is, indeed, the way of beauty and good, that all that
is touched by them reflect them back, as a mirror reflects back
light. For several days now— which seem to pass so slowly, as
I wait for the hammer to be fully empowered and placed in
Berto's bed— for several days the Signora Messina has begun
attending not only compline, but lauds as well, and sits with
us when there is shade in the courtyard. Though we are forbidden to speak with her except when absolutely necessary,
this is the rule applying to all residents of the house among
themselves, and so though the Signora's magnificence strikes
us with a consciousness of our lowliness, her presence does
not really disturb us. When she sits with us in the courtyard,
she reads, silently, from a book she holds in her lap, while the
rest of us spin or sew or weave, and some of us sing hymns or
other songs to which the matron can find no objection. The
day before yesterday the matron, annoyed by our singing
(though I do not understand it, except that I think she believes it is her duty to be sure we are all miserable and sober
and gloomy, so that our punishment in being here is as oppressive as possible), requested Signora Messina to read aloud
to us from her book. The Signora looked at the matron, lifted
one of her very fine, silken brows, and then smiled slightly.
"It is in Latin," she said. "Will anyone understand it if I read
it aloud?"

Did the dottore teach her Latin, or choose her as his wife
because she had been schooled in it in her father's house?

The Signora said also, "But if you like, I will read to you
tomorrow, from a book in the vernacular." And I remembered
observing when I assisted Mona Gentile in curing the
Signora's whites, that she had a number of books in
her possession.

So yesterday morning the Signora opened her book, saying, "This was written by the famous cardinal of Pope Leo X,
Pietro Bembo." And then she read and read and read, even
when her throat grew dry and she required water, and in the
late afternoon read again, and came to the passage of such
great beauty that even thinking about it now makes my eyes
fill with tears of joy and pleasure. The subject of the reading
was love, of all things (which greatly embarrassed the prostitutes, who profess a great cynicism about love between men
and women). "Surely, if our parents had not loved one another, we would not be here or anywhere else," the Signora
read. "Nor, ladies, does love merely bring human beings into
existence, but it gives a second life as well— or should I rather
call it their principle life— that is the life of virtue, without
which it would perhaps be better not to have been born or
better to have died at birth." This is beautiful and wise, but
the next part is astonishing! "For men would still be wander-
ing up and down the mountains and the woods, as naked, wild
and hairy as the beasts, without roofs or human converse or
domestic customs, had love not persuaded them to meet together in a common life. Then abandoning their cries and
bending their glad tongues to speech, they came to utter their
first words. Little by little, as men lived in this new way, love
gathered strength, and with love grew the arts. For the first
time fathers knew their own children from those of other men.
Villages were newly filled with houses, and cities girt themselves
with walls for defense, and laws were made to guard praisewor-
thy customs. Then friendship, which clearly is a form of love,
began to sow its hallowed name through lands already civilized."

When the Signora finished reading, I begged her to lend
me the book, for though I did not say so, I wanted to learn
that passage by heart, so that I would always have that beauty
within me, forever. The Signora at first looked surprised, then
murmured, "But you are Mona Gentile's apprentice, are you
not. Naturally she has taught you to read."

Because some made sly comments about that beautiful passage, the matron coarsely reminded us that not long ago Don Alessandro preached a sermon to us about the Fall, about how God gave Adam and Eve everything, and for her insatiable curiosity and lust, Eve ruined it all— yes, lust, for why else must we learn shame after her sin, which compelled our first parents to put on fig leaves afterwards.

But we could all see, so clearly before us, the nobility and worth of the Signora Messina, whose hands are as delicate and white as her face, whose collar and coif-cloth, even on this ordinary day, were of fine spotlessly white lace, and whose dress was so exquisitely stitched with bands of silk, her skirts and petticoats so richly full and stiff. And this lady looked utterly calm and unperturbed at Francesca's aspersions, knowing as she did that such a one could never offer any kind of reproach to her. She responded firmly, yet easily: "Pope Leo X thought highly of Cardinal Bembo, who wrote those words." And Adriana tittered, and said maybe so, but her first lover, at thirteen, had been the priest she made her confessions to. At which the matron imposed silence on us, so that the Signora was able to resume reading aloud.

Mona Gentile yesterday sent the message by the portress that she earlier told me would indicate that the hammer had been fully empowered and placed under Berto's bed. And so last night, very late, I undertook the most dangerous part of my mission. I took the sealed heart of the bird wrapped in the remains of Berto's shirt and lay with it pressed to my breast, and then withdrew my spirit from my body. It frightened me a little, abandoning my body defenseless, knowing that if anyone were to come in and move it that I should perish. All previous times I had done it with Mona Gentile watching over it, as I have done for her. Yet I felt a great exhilaration to find myself flying out into the Via del Galliera, and from thence to the Via Asse and into the house of Berto's father. It has been so long since I've been out of this house, so long since I have seen anything but plain gray walls! Yet suddenly I could go where I wanted, without hindrance, knowing that I would meet only other spirits, that no one embodied could see me! Of course I did not want to meet other spirits, for often they get themselves into mischief, or engage in terrible battle, as the Benandanti, wielding fennel stalks, do against witches. Happily, though, I met no other spirits, and though I enjoyed lingering in the rooms of Berto's father's house, which are filled with fine furniture, tapestries, and many books more than Ser Achille himself owns, the desire to see Berto filled me with an urgency to fly to him with all speed and dispatch.

Berto was lying on his side, sleeping. After I made sure the hammer was placed as Mona Gentile had said it would be, I summoned his spirit, which regarded me in great surprise and confusion. Since Berto had been born without the caule, his spirit lacked the power to rise apart from his body, and so was only the faintest bit evident, trapped as it was in flesh.

"My love," I addressed the spirit, as though it were Berto himself. "You will not remember my visit when you awaken, but you will know, deep within your soul, that I have come to you to urge you to keep your promise to me, to make public your having taken me for your wife. I forbid you to take your flesh to any other, I forbid you any pleasure in your member until you have kept your word to me. A promise is a promise, and no one could make you a better wife than I, who adore and know how to please you, and who will soon be bearing your child. Until you keep your promise to me, you will take no refreshment from your sleep, and will dream only of me, and how you now deny the one you once called wife. Sleep now, Berto. But remember, in the morning, that I am your wife."

So great was my delight in seeing my beloved that I remained for some time to look on his face and form, which in sleep resemble those of an angel, until I recalled how defenseless my own sleeping body truly was, lying in my bed in the Casa del Soccorso. Today I can think of nothing but how much I would have loved to have stroked his face with my carnal hand, as I could not, visiting him only in the spirit.

But he will come to me, of that I am certain. It cannot be long now!

We are all in an uproar in this house. The president of the Congregation and Don Anselmo and several members, including the Signor Dottore Segnelli, have been here, to question all of us, and to send the matron and portress away altogether! They have named Mona Elissa as the new matron and appointed Silvestra Leli to be portress.

It happened this morning, after breakfast, that the Signora Messina and I were both coming down the stairs at the same time, I carrying my work basket, she three books and a silk, gold thread-embroidered pouch. When we reached the foot of the stairs, she hesitated, and I thought at first she intended to use the privy, but then she said to me that she wished to have a word with the portress. This surprised me, for usually she did not deign to notice that woman. And so I supposed that the Signora intended to bribe her to carry a message outside. Shamelessly I lingered, out of curiosity (though I did not tell the signori that!), to see if Mona Antonia could be bribed. But what happened was this: when the Signora had almost reached the portress's bench, she dropped her books. While the Signora exclaimed loudly, the portress bent over, to pick them up. And quickly, to my astonishment, the Signora raised the pouch high over her head and then brought it down with great force and violence on the portress's head! The portress gasped, and collapsed. The Signora then unbarred and unbolted the door, and glancing over her shoulder, saw me standing there, and so called softly to me to escape with her, if I liked!

Oh the tightness in my chest at that moment! Oh the tears choking my throat and prickling my eyelids! The thought of freedom was sweet— but even without a moment's reflection I knew that the cost would be too high. I would lose everything if I fled, I would lose Berto, I would lose Mona Gentile, I would lose all chance of restoring my honor. If I fled, I would either end up in the Casa della Probazione, or as the meanest whore on the streets— and so far advanced in my pregnancy, too! So I shook my head, to let her know that I would not go. And then the doorway stood empty.

I knelt by Mona Antonia, who was groaning. Her eyelids fluttered, and then opened, and then closed again as a great moan issued from her. I lingered at her side, so as to delay going to the matron, who I knew would set up a great hue and cry. But when I saw a trickle of blood coming out of Mona Antonia's nose, I knew that I must get help for her at once, and ceased to delay.

I do not know if they will apprehend the Signora. If she has money and people who will help her despite her husband's wishes, she will probably escape. Everyone here is both excited and gloomy. It will be dull again here without the Signora's beauty and finery to lighten our days. And we can all guess that Mona Elissa will be harsh in enforcing her piety on us. Catarina whispered to me as we were entering the chapel for compline that we will be lucky if she doesn't start making us get up in the middle of night for matins!

I have been so dull, and have been so oppressed with the burden of pregnancy, that I haven't felt any desire to chatter, much less write in this little book. Mona Gentile says that Berto is suffering greatly— that he seems to be literally wasting away. He has no appetite. A doctor was called and said that he lacked sufficient heat (which he said was probably caused by dissipated living). The doctor bled him, and purged him, and gave him an emetic, and put him on a strict regimen.

Every now and then I send my spirit to Berto, to bid him to keep his promise. How can he be so stubborn? I do not understand it, since to keep his word to me will bring him everything that is good, while resistance is making him ill, and less than a man.

It is sad. But my love will prevail and be justified.

"You must decide how far you want to go," Mona Gentile told me this morning. Angelica, the servant she bribed, came to her, deeply distressed by Berto's debilitation. She wishes the hammer removed because she thinks Berto may die of it.

These words, when Mona Gentile conveyed them to me, struck terror deep into my heart. Surely he will not die! I said to her, begging her reassurance. But Mona Gentile said, "He has indeed become ill. His spirit is resisting the hammer, and may even resist it unto death. It may be that the love, or even desire, that you wished to bind no longer existed at the time you made the hammer. If there is no love, nor even desire, the spirit cannot be compelled, though it dies resisting your will to bind it."

Do I wish Berto to die? No, a thousand times no! Though I am sometimes angry at him for having abandoned me, his promised wife, I am a woman, not a man who would rather see his beloved dead than leave him. Unwomanly revenge could never be my way.

And so, Mona Gentile says, I must either decide to release him, or go to the Devil, that he may be inspired with the love that he no longer feels. But if I go to the Devil for such a purpose, it will cost me dearly. It will cost me, no doubt, my soul. For the Devil never performs such arduous feats but for the ultimate price.

I ponder these things. A few months ago, before I began to contemplate the risks of childbed, I might have cast my soul to the winds, to win Berto to me. I can think of nothing more important to me! And yet— when I think of how I may well perish in the struggle to be delivered of this child, I feel fearful for my immortal soul.

Don Tomaso has warned that in the practice of magic one must be careful not to endanger her soul. When I threw the pinch of salt into the fire today, not only the Devil's eyes, but most of his face manifested itself to my sight. My heart almost failed when I saw it, and I trembled so violently I collapsed right there in the kitchen and had to be assisted by Catarina, who being a silly fearful thing, believed I was beginning my pains. Fear has become my shadow. For I do not know what I will do. I cannot face losing Berto, either to death, or to his indifference. But do I wish to lose my soul to regain him? Alas! I must be the most unhappy woman alive!

If Mona Elissa was a disagreeable old scold before, she is now an insufferable tyrant. Daily she rages at all of us— and lately I've become the favorite target of her fury. Yesterday when I nodded over my spindle, she shrieked at me that I should not be sitting about idle, that a "strapping great girl like me" ought to be doing all the hardest work in the house, instead of none at all. And it especially annoys her that I have become so large and clumsy that I need help getting up from my knees in chapel. "Putting on airs, as though noble and delicate blood flows through your veins, when you and I both know your mother worked in the fields through all her pregnancies. You are nothing but a concubine who got herself dismissed for getting pregnant. Idleness is not for such as you!" And though Ser Achille pays the full "extraordinary" board for me, and the Signora Consolini would be angry to hear of it, Mona Elissa persists in trying to put me to work with the residents too poor to pay maintenance. But it's obvious she hates the Signora Consolini— and since the Signora Messina's escape has loudly proclaimed that the Congregation put her in charge, that members' wives have no authority in the house, and that many of them are no better than they should be.

Other examples of her officiousness: last week when Anna and Angela quarreled over whose turn it was to clean out the chamber pots in the dormitory, and not only screamed invectives at one another but began hair-pulling and other sorts of disorderly behavior typical of whores, Mona Elissa went and fetched the cudgel the Congregation gave to the new portress so as to prevent any further escapes, and beat both women about the shoulders and haunches, in a rage at their creating disorder in this house, which she called "honest."

And then today she came in here to inspect my room, to see that it was "in order." When she saw the one book that I own, a gift from Don Tomaso, she demanded to know what it was. When I told her it was *Il Legendario de Santi*, she was suspicious, as though she thought I might be lying to her, and opened it at random and ordered me to read from it. The page she opened to was a description of the martyrdom of Saint Perpetua. Talk about fury! That one, it turns out, was enraged that a book should praise that saint, who Mona Elissa said was a shameful example to all decent women, for having deserted her husband and child and disobeyed her parents for the glory of martyrdom, because she was so full of herself. Clearly Mona Elissa can have no respect for any of the women saints, since no woman, other than Mary, was ever sainted for bearing children and being a good wife and daughter!

And then she saw this little book, and seeing that it had script in it asked me what it was. I said that it was a book Don Tomaso had given me for making observations on my devotional progress. (That is what such little notebooks are usually used for, and since Mona Elissa cannot read, I did not fear my lie being exposed.) Mona Elissa snorted, and said that it was a bad thing, making women too full of their own importance, there being so many women these days writing at their confessors' request, and taking their souls so seriously, which had previously not been necessary, when simply going to Mass and confession and saying one's prayers sufficed.

Soon Mona Gentile will come, and I will have to give her my decision. Time is running out— both for Berto, and for me, since my labor will begin any day now. I fear it is not a good thing to send my spirit out from my body when the baby is so active and lively within me. And yet, before I can make my decision, I must speak with Berto's spirit. I must know why he has spurned me. Perhaps it is because his father has forbidden him, or his mother has made him promise to break his word to me.

I wish for a sign, to tell me what I must do. No method of divination I have tried yet has given me one. I pray that this night will show me the way.

I would not have believed it was possible to be more unhappy than I have been these past months that I have been living in this house. Nor would I ever have believed it possible that the spirit of vengeance and outrage, such as that motivates men to kill their own wives and other men when their honor is threatened, could move me. And yet both these things have come to pass. Oh miserable girl, who thinks now of the Devil, lurking in the hearth, eager to become her lord, though he is such a low, mean creature, who must skulk in out of the way places, such a miserable power who has never had even one altar raised to him, much less a church. . .

The pain in my breast is a coldness, that makes all of my body ache with the most forsaken emptiness. And this though my breasts and womb are full past belief!

I parted my spirit from my body last night and flew to the Via Asse to see Berto. An old woman sat at his bedside, continually replacing wet cloths on his head which, his head whipping constantly about, were again and again dislodged. His breathing was harsh and difficult, full of hoarse cries and whimpers such as I have never heard. His face was pale and wasted, and his eyes, which were open, stared wildly about, without apparently seeing anything. My heart was wrung with pity and remorse for what I had brought on him.

I almost left his bedside then, determined to free him from the power of my hammer. But I could not refrain from speaking to his spirit, certain, as I was, that it would be the last time we met, face to face. So I summoned his spirit, and bidding it speak truthfully— which it could not help but do, since it was obeying my summons— I demanded of him whether any trace of love for me remained in his heart.

The spirit laughed raucously and shrilly, as though untouched by the weakness of the body it inhabits. "Love!" it scoffed. "I set out to give you the trick, and I succeeded. I even made a wager with Rico, that I would. I possessed you for months— and now will even get a child from you! What a fool you were, thinking you could snare the son of a high magistrate with your body, thinking that the man whose mother is the daughter of a long line of noted bankers would throw his family's magnificent honor away on you, you with generations of mud under your fingernails, your father and his father before him bred like oxen for the fields. You! You are nothing! Nothing!"

(*Sei niente! Niente!*)

Though my body lay some distance away, it was as though Berto had plunged a knife into my heart. But even more than the pain, I burned with a sudden frigid anger, like a piece of smoking ice within my belly, for never even in my darkest moments had I believed Ser Achille, or the truth of the terrible dream, that my beloved had deliberately set out to give me the trick. Nothing, he called me. And the word reverberated in me, and it seemed to me that I was indeed nothing, a hollow being, whose spirit would blow away now that her heart had been stolen from her.

I do not know what happened then. A kind of red mist obscures my memory, I only remember later, lying in my bed, plotting Berto's destruction, plotting his father's destruction, plotting even the destruction of his mother's so-magnificent kinsmen. The Devil could be summoned, he was nearby. This thought rang through my mind, like a bell that will not be silenced. Like a bell tolling a death. Like the bell of doom.

I dozed a little. Later, during lauds, I thought about the consequences of doing such great business with the Devil. In that little chapel, our Lord Jesus looks pathetic hanging on his cross. And so as I knelt, facing the crucifix, the words of Antonio, the journeyman of the baker in the Via Sarogozza, came to me, arguing that Jesus was too powerless to have been a real lord, or he would not have been crucified, but was just the illegitimate son of a cuckolded carpenter, and that there is no hell, for there is no heaven, because there is only death, and then nothing. And yet— I kept thinking, in argument with myself— the Devil is even less impressive, and commands no respect at all, anywhere. What truly powerful lord lurks about, waiting for even the meanest of servants to summons him, to do business?

The initial fierceness of my rage has cooled, leaving me doubtful that I want to exchange my soul for vengeance. Still, what joy it would bring me to triumph over Berto, to command his every obedience, even if it meant incurring his eternal hatred! I was willing to do anything to please him— and I did— but that for love, for which he now scorns me, as though love were worthless.

Per dio. I wish Mona Gentile had come today. I am tired, and sick, of the tolling of that bell in my head. I could die in childbed tonight, or tomorrow, or the next day. And if I pledge my soul to the devil, I could be in hell before I even saw my vengeance carried out.

By the blessed tears of Jesus, this book of mine is a near ruin. A great storm came in the night and because I had left the shutters open on account of the terrible close heat, the rain poured into the room, soaking my little book, as well as my *Legendario de Santi.* The printed book is not nearly as soaked, because the leather of its covers protected it; and though some of its pages are damp, and far more costly than the cheap paper of my little book, they will dry unscathed. My little book, though, is a disgrace. The soot I have been using for ink smeared over the pages horribly, blurring my already ugly hand. Even as I write now with such difficulty because of the dampness of the paper, I see my writing as Ser Achille himself would see it: ugly, misshapen, a blur of soot marring what was once good (if cheap) clean paper.

It strikes me, like a sign: if writing is the mirror of the soul, then mine is misshapen and deformed, a veritable blot on Creation.

Love— yes, today, it is on my mind. I was reminded of the passage I learned by heart, read to us by the Signora Messina. To think of it redoubles my pain. We made a child, Berto and I, a child he will own. And yet— what of love? The only love was mine, and that was a delusion, conceived, birthed, and nursed by him.

And still— I feel in my heart, which is otherwise a cold hollow thing, the beauty of the love there described. I am nothing, my love simply derisory, according to Berto. Perhaps. But perhaps, too, it is simply that Berto's soul is too small, or I wholly unworthy of inspiring love in anyone. Is my soul truly so deformed as this little book now tells me? Is it as good as given to the Devil, whatever I decide? What is the meaning of the sign that this little book has given me? What does it mean that even as I scrawl on these damp pages, the writing blurs into stains and lumps of soot?

And now I write one last time in this book, to make it complete, before burning it in the fire, to make pure what has been vile and ugly.

When Mona Gentile came to me today I related to her all that Berto's spirit had said to me, and told her how I had thrown the bird's heart into the kitchen fire and released Berto from the hammer. Mona Gentile then embraced me as tenderly as I have ever known her to do and kissed my cheeks many times, saying that she was gratified, and happy at my decision. Her eyes became bright, and shone with emotion, and even filled with tears of wonderful sincerity. I was surprised, because she had never said that releasing Berto would please her, and asked her why she hadn't. "There are some lessons that cannot be taught, but only learned through experience," she said. "Many are the women who become so possessed by the desire to be desired, that they lose the whole world in their effort to achieve it. There is nothing to be done for those so possessed. Nothing else can matter to them, and indeed the world is lost to them. You have learned now for yourself that sometimes our spells to bind have the effect of binding us, who cast them, just as closely and relentlessly as those we seek to bind. Magic is strong and powerful. And now we know that you are strong enough and powerful enough to become a master of it."

And though my heart did not cease to be bitterly grieved and bruised, yet Mona Gentile's rejoicing, and her teaching me a lesson I had not known I was learning, filled up the emptiness that Berto's spirit had hollowed out when he said that I was nothing.

I am ready to become a healer, Mona Gentile says. And there is nothing more powerful that any woman can be, except for queens and consorts of dukes and princes. That is, I know, true. Only what of love, I wonder? What of the great thing called love which has civilized man?

When I asked Mona Gentile, she smiled, and patted my hand, and said "Child, this is not a question for a girl of seventeen years to ask. Be patient. And perhaps, when you are twice your years, you will be able to tell me."

And so goodbye, little book, goodbye. Our time together is over.

Lord Enoch's Revels

1.

The town car glides to a stop a few yards from Lord Enoch's garden gate. Sibyl, Baroness Sylvan, stares at the flames loosely streaming from the torches flanking the gate and wonders what she could possibly have been thinking to have come here. Her hands may be gloved in silk, but they tremble. Her heart, broken only seven months' past, hasn't even begun to heal. She touches the gloved tips of her fingers to her lips. She's enough of a woman of experience to know that a party hosted by a stranger is no place for her kind of wound. But the porter steps away from the gate and opens the back door of the car; the bowing of his claret-liveried body mimics deference.

Sibyl's aubergine lace rustles and pulls and almost rips as she slides over the seat and steps out of the car. She masks her face with hauteur as she hands the porter her invitation and passes quickly through the gate. Inside, the garden smells of jasmine and burning pitch. She glimpses a rabbit peering at her from between the feathery stalks of a bed of ornamental asparagus. Some dark, mysterious force draws her on. Although her pulse flutters with excited dread, she does not allow herself to look back.

2.

Who has not heard wild, extravagant tales recounting the lavishness of Lord Enoch's hospitality? Those who have experienced it will say only that behind the lord's walls the supply of wine is infinite, the guests dance through the night, and every chamber in the castle is put generously at the guests' disposal. They do not say that the lord's gilt-edged invitations command that each guest bidden to the revels arrive alone, or that most guests will be expelled from the grounds without warning while the party continues on without them. They speak only to praise the lord and the beauty to be found within his walls.

Do not imagine that Lord Enoch's guests consciously censor themselves. Be certain, rather, that they remain silent for lack of words to express what they know they do not even begin to understand.

3.

In the gardens the wine flows from two fountains. From the silver fountain foams a crisp, delicious champagne, while from the gold fountain spurts a rich-bodied, almost black syrah. The musicians pause only to allow couples to change partners; they play for hours without breaking. Sibyl lives within her body and forgets everything but the moment. She is barely aware that although she hasn't been introduced to a single other guest, she is never alone and that when she is not dancing she's either flooding her mouth with wine or is down on the ground with her current partner. She does notice, though, that couples frequently disappear into the castle, no longer contented, she assumes, to roll in the grass (which is damp and jumping with ticks). Each glimpse she snatches of couples slipping away stabs her breast with painful memory, but always the ache dissolves under the touch of her partner's lips, tongue, and hands, under the beat of the tambourine, under the poignant whine of the fiddle.

Time passes and passes, but for Sibyl it's only one long, sultry night of the body, as she dances and fucks and drinks beneath a cloudless, moonless sky.

4.

Lord Enoch is everywhere, moving constantly among his guests, crying welcome, slipping around the couples dancing, his eyes gleaming and blessing those fucking in the grass. Lord Enoch is nowhere, beyond encounter, the invisible host of the revels who seems to want nothing for himself but his guests' intense and constant pleasure.

What does Lord Enoch actually want?

Nobody knows.

But then nobody asks, either.

5.

Sibyl reels drunkenly through the passages of the castle's north and east wings. On the other side of every door she opens she finds Lord Enoch's guests either pursuing passion or alone and weeping. So many large, voluptuous thighs flash in the occasional patch of lamplight like strawberry yogurt, so many goatishly hairy buttocks rear high in the air. Dark genital smells seep through the castle's passages, and for the moments that Sibyl remains alone she wallows in a furtive and lonely sadness. She can't remember entering the castle. A partner, she supposes, must have brought her there.

But the moments of solitude pass, and Sibyl is swept into an elaborate practice of passion as complex and precise as a knot theorist's fondest construction. The music in the garden can be heard in the distance, a stealthy engine that tunnels under the walls and rises like heat to join the scents that travel from room to room, passage to passage, saturating the very air the castle's guests must breathe.

6.

Outdoors in the garden, the long flames of the torches flare violently, as though the flow of fuel to each had suddenly doubled. A long, continuous roll of kettledrums replaces the dance music, innocuous until the almost imperceptible rhythm of the roll penetrates the guests' bodies, pounding upwards through the soles of their feet, slaving their heart-beats, roaring in their ears, tickling the nerves in their groins. The drum roll impels each guest to enter the castle alone, partners all forgotten. Lord Enoch stands with his back to the "still life" painted in the manner of Soutine that hangs in the gallery overlooking his enormous Great Hall. He drinks in the spectacle of his guests flowing in through the double doors below, their limbs easy with grace (though they have been struck as silent as zombies), each obeying the beat of the drums, the beat of their hearts, the beat of the desire their many and varied couplings have stoked rather than slaked. At the far end of the Great Hall they begin the descent, down the steep, single flight of 839 stairs. Lord Enoch's spirit soars as down, down, they go, down into the stone chambers that lay stories and stories below, some of the guests joyful, others sad and weeping, the passion consuming them an open, bleeding wound such a night must break open rather than stanch.

What does Lord Enoch want? Certainly he wants his guests to tread every one of his 839 steps, down, and down, and down into the bowels of his grand castle. *Oh sweetness, such sweetness* one can easily imagine him saying.

7.

Sweetness, yes, for Sibyl, Baroness Sylvan, a sweetness that squeezes her throat, that shapes itself into a lump pressing down on her chest. She wanders the caves lush with kudzu, where wine drips from the ceiling into mouths opened by the moans of orgasm. She is lost and alone, the Baroness Sylvan, even when caught up in others' embrace. But many and many of the guests are lost, alone in the sweetness, indifferent to everything, even their own pleasure. Sibyl can only ache and long for her lost lover as the wine drips into her mouth, as the night never ends, as the music holds her in thrall.

8.

Lord Enoch savors the night's gifts. One by one his guests find themselves in the cold and the dark, alone outside the garden walls. The castle, the walls, and the gardens dissolve into mist, as if they had never been. Sibyl had been longing to leave, but cast out from the revels she falls to her knees, submissive to the lash of despair.

Inside, the night goes on and on, with wine that never stops flowing, with music that never falls silent, with an interior space that never stops growing.

And Lord Enoch is pleased.

For two centuries a feminist has been a woman who does not leave others to think for her, whether it be a question simply of thinking or, more particularly, thinking about the feminine condition or what it should be. If we make a link (at least as a hypothesis) between thinking philosophically and self-assertion through thought, or the individual withdrawal from generally held beliefs, then "thinking philosophically" and "being a feminist" appear as one and the same attitude: a desire to judge by and for oneself, which may manifest itself in relation to different questions.

—Michéle Le Doeuff, *Hipparchia's Choice: An Essay Concerning Women, Philosophy, Etc.*

The Héloïse Archive

27 February, 1848
Dr. Carline ("the Provocative") of Meaux
Margaret of Flanders Institute of the Philosophical Sciences
The Hague

Dear Professor Carline:

Perhaps you will recall our recent encounter. If not, permit me to remind you that we spoke briefly at the reception following a talk you presented here at the Sorbonne (Spring 1845). It was titled "Has/Does the Future Manipulate(d) the Past?", awkwardly, it seemed at the time, but— as I now believe— appropriately.

I have recently had reason to recall your talk. One of our graduate students, Aletis of Nogent-sur-Seine, has been working in a little-known (and previously unmined) archive from Troyes, Champagne, that was acquired by the Bibliothèque Historique (Paris) at the turn of the century, but never properly indexed or even comprehensively surveyed for its contents. It has fallen to Aletis's lot, by default, to perform these basic library tasks. In the course of sorting and listing the contents, Aletis came upon an extraordinary set of documents. (She cannot entirely account for her pausing to read them, but I'm certain anyone with archival experience will recognize how the idle impulse of curiosity constantly tempts scholars to tarry over items irrelevant to their work.) The documents are one side of a 12th-century correspondence. The first two letters, while articulating an unusual degree of

emotional consciousness and turmoil, are otherwise unre-
markable. The fifteen remaining letters, however, are extraordinary for being filled with references that would be
incomprehensible (or simply the marks of delusion)— to
anyone, that is, who had not heard your talk.

I will, of course, leave it to you to evaluate the references
for yourself.

You will convey my apologies, I hope, to your Institute's
staff for my having inconvenienced them by faxing this batch
of materials under the "Special Privacy Handling" status. If
my speculation is correct, all due care must be taken that
the contents of the documents not be disseminated to the
public prematurely.

Respectfully,
Claude ("the Mordant") of Basel
Director of Humanistic Sciences
Sorbonne, Paris

P.S. You will find in this fax batch not only copies of the
originals, but also a transcription and translation of them into
modern French (abridged of numerous lengthy passages citing a variety of classical, biblical, and patristic sources char-
acteristic of the writing of 12th-century educated persons)
provided for your convenience. At my request Aletis has sup-
plied explanatory material in footnotes where she deemed
them essential for making the text comprehensible to a non-
specialist. She has also made notations about the language
used in the original text of which someone reading only the
translation might wish to be cognizant.

Shrine of disappointed love.
Tomb of Héloïse and Abelard.
Courtsey the Charles Deering McCormick Library of Special
Collections, Northwestern University Library
Evanston, Illinois

Letter 1 (ca. 1133)

[To] him who is especially her lord, [from] she who is uniquely his: to Abélard from Héloïse:[1]

You must know already from your man that your letter reached me safely last month. Beloved, my bowels turned to water as I read it. Indeed, I spent two days so distraught and pain-stricken that, avoiding all duties and obligations, I kept to my cell, refusing to see anyone at all. There I argued long with myself, struggling to reclaim the numb peace I had formerly made with the intolerable. For a month now I have been thinking about and reasoning with your letter and, with my sisters, praying to God the more frequently for your safety, hardly eating, stopping only to perform the Offices and the most pressing of my duties, and to greet guests of rank.

Always we hold the deepest concern for your health and safety, and— as you must have expected— shuddered to read afresh of your monks' attempts to take your life. Indeed, the terrible fear perpetually haunts me, that word of your death at the hands of your enemies will be brought to me, shattering what little peace of mind I can ever find, such that I would be sent swiftly following you, out of a life I should no more have the will to bear. It is an occasion too easy for me to imagine, since I continue to remember with the utmost vividness those moments in which I, summoned to the refectory at Argenteuil, received word from the mother abbess of your mutilation. You will, I know, be pleased that the sisters of the Paraclete pray continuously for your safety, strictly following your instructions. For years I have grieved at the unspeakable price you paid for our love and told myself that I must accept my own burden of sorrow likewise, and with grace, lest I dishonor you.

Oh love. You must know that my heart leaped with joy when your letter was first put into my hand. You had not, after all, written me since your last visit here. And when I

¹ Abélard (b. 1079, near Nantes) was a noted theologian, philosopher, teacher, and composer in his own right, though we now tend to think of him primarily in reference to Héloïse (b. 1100 or 1101), the great philosopher, theologian, and scholar, and the principal founder of the Magdalenian Reform that first swept Europe in the mid-12th century. At the time Héloïse wrote this letter, she was the acting abbess of the Paraclete, a religious house she founded (with Abélard's assistance) in 1129. The personal history to which she alludes in this first letter can be summarized thus: famous for her erudition when she at age sixteen left Ste. Marie of Argenteuil, the convent where she was educated, Héloïse went to live with her uncle, Fulbert, in the cloister of Notre Dame in Paris (where he was a canon); Abélard, himself lionized by five thousand students (most of whom paid fees to him directly), arranged to take lodging with Fulbert in exchange for paying a nominal amount of rent and tutoring Héloïse. During the course of their lessons, they became lovers; Héloïse became pregnant, and retreated to Abélard's family's chateau to have the baby. When she returned to Paris, married Abélard, and took up residence again in Argenteuil, her uncle, considering her safe from retaliation by Abélard's family, had him castrated. Both Héloïse and Abélard then took holy orders (in 1119, according to extant monastic records), Héloïse to live cloistered, Abélard to return to teaching. Abélard soon ran into trouble, however, and was summoned before the Council of Soissons to be censured for heresy, probably because his work on St. Denis undermined royal efforts to claim the saint as patron. He was briefly confined in a monastic prison and then allowed to teach in the "wilderness" of Champagne until forced to accept an appointment as abbot to a house of monks, some of whom made several attempts to assassinate him, apparently in retaliation for his efforts to reform them. When in 1129 the powerful Abbè Suger ejected the nuns from their convent at Argenteuil where Héloïse was prioress, Abélard offered her the Paraclete (which he had crudely constructed a few years earlier). The result was the founding of not only a new religious house, but also the Order of the Paraclete (later renamed the Magdalene), which Héloïse quickly built up during her highly successful years as abbess.

saw how it began, I believed that at last I would see our tragic history set forth and the full truth of the events that befell us set down in some sensible order that would bring comfort to my spirit and discipline to my mind. But after many days' struggle to come to terms with the harshness of its language, I continue so heart-sickened by your letter that I hardly know how to begin replying to— or shall it be disputing? — it. Tell me, dearest, how I am to read it. You say in the only slightly more personal note accompanying it that you wrote it both to console me and to set forth an account that would "clarify" matters for your friends, pupils, and superiors.

Perhaps I should make a point by point refutation— where you have led me to believe one thing, and here stated another, or simplified the complex into distorted meaninglessness, or passed over in silence the definingly important, all of which add up to a lie of excruciating proportions. Was it not you, my only love, who used often to declare that we were one flesh with joined spirits, such that lying to one another would be the same as lying to our own selves or to God? Am I to understand from your letter that you wish me to erase from memory all that is written in my soul and stamped on my heart and replace it with lies?

And what did you mean, praising me for my "reputed holiness"? Even during mass, the phantasms of ecstatic pleasure, burned by you into my brain, never cease to captivate me. I have told you often enough what I find it worth bruising my knees for. The cell is the only place where I can be assured of solitude and privacy to review the past and ease my lust as best I can, which is all you have left to me, you who withdrew all your love when your lust died. It means nothing that men judge me chaste and religious, for as everyone knows, there is little religion remaining that is not hypocrisy, when the highest praise is awarded only to those who take care not to offend the opinions of the powerful.

You are the greatest, wisest man alive, beloved, and you have been (and remain) my lord and master.[2] But never is pupil, vassal, or servant to submit silently to what their reason tells them is foolishness and lies. Though you write to the contrary in your *Ethics*, this you once taught me, too, despite your often saying now that the weaker sex should not speak at all.[3] And so I must answer you, my lord. Yes, you have suffered sorely— your account of all the grief and burden and trials God has put upon you made me weep as bitterly as the hurtfulness of the lies about us did. But still, in the name of all we have ever been to one another, I demand that you abide by our covenant. Remember, beloved: it was our covenant that commanded my every obedience to your will, however harsh its significance for me. Because of it I allowed you to bind me twice in formal rituals that we both know have little to do with the reason and feeling of the heart. But what use is a covenant if one party can abrogate its terms simply at will?

In your letter you speak freely of the premeditation of your seduction of me. Reading your cool, scornful statements, my thoughts flew back to that day when I watched from the window of my uncle's house, as you and the crowd of students surrounding you, each hanging on your least word, emerged from your school, and your eyes lifted to my window and met mine over their heads, causing me to blush and avert them from your powerful gaze. You later told me that

---

[2] The Latin is *dominus et magister.* Abélard, as an abbot, would correctly be addressed as *dominus.* (And in fact priests were commonly addressed so, too, and Abélard was of course a priest.) *Magister* was roughly the equivalent of our university professor, and must certainly have been his title at least since his appointment to the faculty of the prestigious cathedral school of Notre Dame. (Note: Cathedral schools were precursors to universities.)

[3] By "weaker sex" she means women. For an explanation, see Elizabeth ("the Jokester") of Chastagnier's *L'Histoire et la Langue de la Misogynie Ancienne* (Lyon: 1677).

you'd conceived an overwhelming passion for me at that moment, prompting you to plot your way into my uncle's household. You easily succeeded at your goal, of course, since my uncle received your offer with the highest exultation, overjoyed by the prospect of having such a great man living under his roof. You say in your letter that you could hardly believe your great good fortune at being asked to teach me at whatever hours of the night and day you chose, and you ridicule my uncle for having told you that you could teach and punish me as you wished. Perhaps this is true, for reading this I recalled how when you first began my lessons you told me my uncle was a fool for bringing a gently-bred girl to live among the rowdy young men of the cathedral close.[4]

[4] In the early 12th century women were not admitted as students at the Cathedral Schools of Western Europe. For most of the feudal period women were educated only in convents, and privately. Only the oldest universities in Western Europe, in Southern Italy, allowed women to study with men. (The university at Salerno, it should be added, had a notable reputation for the presence of women on its faculty of medical arts.)

What I have never understood, and what neither version you have told can explain, is why if you intended from the beginning to seduce me you did everything in your power to make yourself hateful to me those first two months in my uncle's house, why you treated me with a contempt I'd never before (or since) been forced to bear, dragging me from my bed and frightening me into such stuttering inanity our lessons were a pointless torture to me, all the while telling me you thought nothing of my learning (the fame of which you said you'd heard long before meeting me). Do you not know that even after we became lovers the sound of your feet on the stairs in the night would send the breath from my lungs and make my body tremble (and never wholly from desire)? Certainly I for a long time believed that my struggle to maintain my dignity in the face of your persecution gradually melted the hardness of your heart and softened the harshness of your opinion of me. Do you not know that your behavior made me think my uncle had inflicted you

on me because he thought me too proud of my accomplish-
ment, too sure of my mastery of philosophy? I knew of and
admired you even when I was at Argenteuil, for we talked of
you there, since everyone knew yours was the greatest intellect in all of Christendom.

Kneeling in my cell, I often relive that first time you took
me in your arms. That was the night you told me you would
thrash me if I made a single error in the recitation of Juvenal
you set me without advance notice. And of course, because
you were so severe with me, I could not help but make an
error, and so for the first time broke down weeping, mortified
with shame at what must follow. But then instead of punishing me with your rod, you gathered me close and kissed and
stroked my hair and slipping into your softest and most gentle
vernacular called me "sweet" and sang softly in my ear the
first of the many songs you composed for me, while hot tears
drenched my eyes and scalded my cheeks. Only now, beloved,
when I am pleading for truthfulness, do I dare tell you what
I have always wanted to say about our lessons. The warm praise
and gentle, maternal caresses of my teachers at Argenteuil
made me love to learn the beautiful Italiante style of writing, the cadences of which you have yourself on occasion admired in the sentences I pen,[5] as well as Greek and Hebrew—
of which you yourself admit to understanding little— while
your blows and beratements made me, for a time, dread our
lessons and loathe every text you assigned me.

Perhaps it is true, as you say now, that you never felt love
for me, though you used to profess the contrary when you
implored me to trust you. When you said you loved, no adored,
no worshiped me, how could I have believed otherwise, you

[5] Except for certain of the later letters in this collection, Héloïse
generally crafts her sentences so that they end in these metrical
cadences. A comparison of Héloïse's extant letters with Abélard's shows a
greater use of the *tardus* than the *velox* cadence, thus following the "Italianate"
style of Adalbertus, which was new to France in the early 12th century.

being who you were? Still, I must wonder. Is it not possible you deny the love you formerly said you felt because you now hate me for my uncle's sake? I know that the whole world says you were mad with a lust devoid of love for me and that your forcing the veil on me was simply to punish me for having been its object (as much as for having been the provocation for my uncle's attack on you).

Always have I known in my heart that my love for you is so surpassing, and your greatness so superior, that I had no need to ask for more. Love comes freely, or not at all; there is nothing more powerful. And it is, surely, more blessed to love than to be loved. The pain of losing your love (or the illusion of it) is something I can bear. Love may come and go (and does) without reflection on one's soul. But I demand of you, master: how can a covenant be broken without staining the honor and integrity of he who repudiates it?

Love alone would never have sufficed to bend my will to your desire first that we be wed, and later that I take vows. Love, on the contrary, argued that I not allow you to sway me to marriage. Your letter, alas, makes clear you still do not understand my reasons for having opposed it. You run on for pages and pages, presenting what you apparently believe to have been my reasoning, and still miss the point. Marriage was the last thing we either wanted or needed. It could only hurt your reputation and ruin your possibilities for preferment. Living in my uncle's house and the cathedral close, I knew before I met you that for someone with unworldly ambitions marriage can only be a disaster. And I knew, too, from reading the ancient secular texts with you that living in the same household with children must invariably destroy the solitude and freedom of mind so essential to the philosopher. I notice in reviewing my arguments you omitted the words of the wise philosopher Aspasia, who observed that marriage vows cannot force the spirit of chastity on those who are only formally joined in wedlock, which is the best argument against marriage that I know of.

We both knew that those perverse acts that are not especially sinful in fornication are a pollution within the sacra-
ment of marriage. I had already taken a vow to you, my lord.
And within the terms of that vow we lived chastely (though
incontinently). Never have either of us shared the pleasures
of the flesh with anyone else. Why intrude the Church into
our beautiful, perfect relation? Do you remember what you
said to me, when, imploring me to formalize my trust in you,
you proposed our convenant, the reasons you gave to win my
consent? There are three ways in which individuals bind
themselves in sacred, holy commitment, you said: by entering into matrimony and into holy orders, and by swearing
oaths of fealty. The first two are the province of the Church.
To have said marriage vows with the consent of our hearts
would have been to marry in actuality, in the eyes of God,
clandestinely. While to have said them inauthentically would
have been to blaspheme, as would it have been to mimic the
taking of holy orders.

On the other hand, you said, the promise a vassal makes to
his lord when he swears fealty and that the lord makes to the
vassal in return is holy, but not sacramental, and is binding
in the eyes of man and God. And though in structure the oath
of fealty resembles marriage, and though it is often made in
church, in the presence of a priest, its execution is both open
and contingent on the needs and wishes of the lord and the
submission, protection, and enrichment of the vassal. And
therefore on this we modeled our convenant, and I knelt to
you and placed my folded hands in yours and swore to be your
vassal, in symbolization of my trust in you, and your care and
protection of me. Do you not remember, my lord? It was summer and all the rest of Paris asleep. The smell of the river
poured through the window. We were in your room in my
uncle's house, and I almost swooning under the gaze of your
powerful, dark eyes gleaming in the flickering candlelight.
After I spoke my vow you raised my hands (still folded in

yours) to your lips and kissed them. And then you put your thin silver chain around my neck, to wear always under my clothing, so that I would not forget.

This cannot be erased though you write a hundred letters denying it. I will not forget, beloved. Not even if you order me to.

You say our marriage— like your mutilation— was a Divine Mercy, that because of it I am now a bride of Christ (to whom you handed me over, as to an overlord). But it was the marriage, beloved, that destroyed us. The marriage was the work of Satan, not God. Until then, we were innocent. You yourself taught me it is not the deed but the intention of the doer which makes the crime. And in this case our intention (or rather your intention) in taking matrimonial vows had nothing to do with the purity and strength of our love. (Or rather, my love.) On the contrary. In your letter you recall the words I spoke and remark on their prophetic import: "One thing remains at last, that in our mutual ruin, the pain may be no less than the love which proceeded it."

You say in your letter that you were moved by my uncle's shame and rage at your "supreme betrayal" of him by having taken me as your whore. Placating him, you say, was the reason for your decision to marry me. I was away in your family's chateau at Le Pallet and so cannot know the truth of what passed between you. But I wonder now, my only love, did my uncle rage at you that what you had started others would finish? Afterwards, when he was so wroth at our keeping our marriage secret, many and many times he told me I must declare to the world I was married lest I become all men's whore, whether I will it or no.

As God is my witness, I neither expected nor hoped, when I mentioned in a letter to you the trouble I'd been having fending off your sister's husband's advances, that you would hurry back to me, determined to wed. It is true that men see one man's whore as available to all, but as I told you when

you came, I could have handled your sister's brother's husband (whom you had previously forced to swear to protect
me from others). When on your arrival you insisted that we
marry, I admit I was gratified (especially since you were at
the same time angry and disgusted with me for suckling our
baby myself), because it made me believe that you loved me
and caused me to redouble my efforts to dissuade you from it,
since your very bodily safety depended upon it. You even say
it in your account of our story, that as long as I remained at
Le Pallet, a virtual hostage to your family, my uncle did not
dare to lift a hand against you.

You offered me a host of reasons for why we should marry.
You said you did not wish me subject to the abuse of my
uncle— to which I answered that I could remain with the
baby in your family's chateau. And then you said that you
could not bear to be so far distant from me— to which I suggested I live at Argenteuil, and noted that our meetings would
be that much sweeter for long absence. You said then that you
could not bear to think that another man might have me—
and to that I said, wounded, that you could trust me. And
finally you said that my uncle might force a marriage to someone else on me, and that with the passing of the years the
differences in our ages would become horrible to me, who
would still be young and fresh when you had become infirm
and grizzled— as you are now, beloved, when still I love and
desire you, though you are not in that one single way any
longer a physically complete man.

Will I never know the truth of your reason for taking the
step that plunged us into disaster? The thought torments me
that you have never trusted me. I knew, for example, that you
didn't trust me when you insisted I precede you into holy orders— obviously because you feared that I would, like Lot's
wife, hesitate and be lost. Of all things, this pains me most.
Surely you have always known I would do anything you ordered, even follow you into Vulcan's fiery pit, for so great is

my love and so solemn the first vow I made you. And why, I must wonder again, should any of this matter to you, if you did not and do not love me— except, as you now claim, 'in Christ"— why should it matter that I belong to no other man?

But then you never understood, either, the reason for my joy in conceiving your child. I thought that pregnancy would offer a final, indisputable proof to you that my passion equaled your own, since a woman cannot release the seed necessary for conception otherwise.[6] But this escaped you, so disgusted with the idea of my being "overtaken" by the "filth" of "women's concerns" and preoccupied with the possible consequences for this new visibility of our love— as though the songs you wrote to enflame my desire did not make our love known through the length and breadth of the land, as though they were not sung— putting my name on every tongue— in even the smallest, most isolated village.

And then it did come to pass, just as I feared, that once we were married our fortunes took a turn for the worse. My uncle grew increasingly wroth at the spoiling of his pride and plans. Though I never knew what he intended for me, I, like you, believe he entertained the grandest and most

[6] Following the tradition of Galen, educated people of 12th-century Western Europe believed that human conception required the ejaculation of both male and female "semen," which then "mixed" to form a fetus they believed was nourished through pregnancy by the mother's menstrual blood, and after pregnancy by whitened menstrual blood (i.e., breast milk). More commonly, people believed that female desire was a constant, rendering women always sexually available and subject to male will (which was apparently considered of a higher order than mere desire). As Maxine ("the Boldly Brilliant") of Antwerp observed in her immensely generative work *On the Development of Zoological Species* (Paris, 1527), particularly in her elaboration of the physiological and behavioral mechanisms that place control of sexual contact in the hands of females in all infrahuman primates, early human cultures took a difficult situation (i.e., the incongruities of human genital arrangements vis-à-vis bipedality and the loss of the pronounced estrous cycle) and made it worse, by forbidding females to display their genitals as a sign of desire signaling sexual invitation. Thus developed the notion that the female's presence itself signaled sexual invitation (which consequently implied that all women desire all sexual contact offered). That Héloïse openly displays her desire to Abélard and refers to her earlier wish that he know her desire and pleasure to have been genuine underscores the nonmonolithic character of cultural indoctrination.

unrealistic of fantasies concerning my future. And rather than ceasing to abuse me, he harassed and struck me all the more frequently for my swearing to others that I had not married you, until, concerned for my well-being, you felt driven to remove me to Argenteuil, where you put me into nun's habit, thus all the more enraging him, as well as leading to even greater blasphemies on our part than before, which was so much to your taste— then.

In your letter you claim that only your mutilation allowed you to regain control over the intensity and constancy of your lust, and that being rendered incapable was a "Divine Mercy." But this is false. The first breathless madness had already ceased to dominate us. Do you forget that on my return to Paris we resolved to spend less time together, for which reason (more than concern for public report) I went to Argenteuil to live quietly? And so you returned your full attention to teaching and writing. That we could part in that way testifies to our having imposed at least the modicum of control over our passion. And, exactly as we anticipated, our separation made our few meetings all the sweeter and more intense, and our letters the more delightful than any we had yet exchanged.

You decry, now, fucking me against the refectory wall on your visits there, you say now it was a dishonor to the Mother of God, just as you excoriate me for having worn the nun's habit while pregnant and for committing acts of sodomy with you as well as having enjoyed every pleasure we could think of during Lent and the vigils of holy feasts. How am I to accept such apparent pieties from your mouth and pen? Do you remember nothing of what you said there in the refectory, when I first protested and refused to satisfy our passion under such circumstances? Have you forgotten taking my hair in your hands (you do remember me, beloved, when I still had hair, hair that you said you loved as dearly as you loved the sun?) and forcing my head back and back and back, until I thought my neck would snap. . . . And do you not remember invoking the covenant then, dearest?

I must stop, for I am weeping, and my fingers nearly life-less with despair. As I clutch the sobs tightly in my throat so that no one here in the library with me will hear them, I cannot help but remember how you on certain piquant occasions said my tears heightened your passion. I must doubt they would do so now (as I must refrain from even hoping you sent your letter to pain me in order to make an impending pleasure sweeter, in accordance with our past practices in the holy art of love), and so will pause to keep my tears from blurring the ink my pen has already laid on this page.

Beloved: always, always, always you assured me that I would not be the woman who would ruin you, as we know from the ancients happens too often with Great Men. We discussed this at length when together we read Ovid (and yes, when, as you say, your hand strayed often to my breast). I would not ruin you: I swore it to myself, I swore it to you, I swore it to God. Think how I suffer now to reflect on the misery and shame (for you insist that you are shamed by your castration) my uncle has brought to you— through me. Yes, beloved, still I grieve at my having played to your Sampson an unwitting Delilah, ever aware that your worst misfortune of all the many you have suffered came to you because we loved, as you say, "beyond all measure."

Perhaps we did lose ourselves in what you now so contemptuously call *lust.* All desires of a carnal nature may be so labeled, but like pleasure, lust itself, dearest— so you used always to declare— is not inherently displeasing to God. But our passion and pleasures in no way degraded us (for it proceeded out of our overwhelming love, which you once taught me was a reflection of Divine Love), and once the first blush of its intensity had passed, had ceased to interfere with your work. At the time this so-called "Divine Mercy" struck out at you, you had resumed your life of teaching and writing, you had recovered your concentration, content (as you said then) to know that I abided at Argenteuil, ready to receive you at such time as you could spare.

Forgive me, I am repeating myself. I must be fearful you will not read my words with the care you once gave to even the most careless scribble of a note I dared send you; or else grief makes it difficult for me to order my thoughts as I should. I will try to state briefly the rest of what I must say. You write that you had thought you would find a safe and peaceful haven with us at the Paraclete, but that an unjustly propagated scandal circulated here suggesting that you, though a "eunuch" (as you revoltingly name yourself), lingered only because you were still moved by lust for me. Beloved, you know that this is exaggeration. No one took seriously what that old serf thought he saw in the stand of poplars near the mill. And if you had stayed no one would have dared to take his suspicion seriously. This is the sort of rumor so patently baseless that it would have had far less power to hurt you than the scurrilous accusations those two false apostles constantly spread through the countryside and whisper in the ears of the most powerful secular lords. Your real reason for leaving was your rage with me afterwards, a rage I can understand, for it was born of genuine grief and frustration at the circumstances that have overtaken us. (And perhaps a little of it was baseless jealousy of Sister Marie, whose admiration and affection for me somehow vexed you.)

Let me put it plainly, beloved. If you dwelled here as our resident priest and spiritual advisor, you would be safe from all threat of assassination and would be able to pursue your great and important work in peace. You know well that my hand is clear and my grammar excellent; and you know, too, that several of my sisters are accomplished copyists. You do not mention it in your letter, but recent visitors brought us the news that our pope, Innocent, has granted you license to leave your wicked, murderous abbey and teach again where you will. We need you, our founder and true spiritual director, here with us, your handmaidens, whose great satisfaction it would be to serve you. And for myself, I know that no matter how much and how well I serve you, it will never suffice to make up for what you have lost through having loved me.

I do not care, dearest one, what the world thinks of our story. But it matters desperately to me that we not be hypocritical with each other, even though at least one of us is living a great lie in feigning in outer appearance what is truly lacking in the most private recess of her heart. If you bear no affection at all to your vassal in love (she who became wife to you and sister in Christ solely in obedience to your wishes), you still owe her honesty and (at least paternal) affection. Beloved! Demanding, I implore of you, imploring, I demand of you, that you make a just rendering to me of your debt.[7]

[7] It is possible that this is a pun, though that would mean Héloïse was speaking ironically, which is by no means certain. The medieval Church considered husband and wife as owing one another sexual intercourse; clerical courts and theological and legal writers commonly referred to this as "the marriage debt." In fact, Héloïse could have requested (and would likely have been granted) an annulment of her marriage by the Church on the grounds that Abélard was incapable of fulfilling the marriage debt.

At one time, when your desire for taking pleasure with me utterly possessed you, your letters came thick and fast. I beg of you, think of our covenant, and what you owe your vassal; give ear to my plaints and pleas, and I will end this long letter with brevity: farewell, my only love.

Postscript: If you would be so good as to tell me what news you have of our son, I would be grateful. You must know that I have heard nothing of him since your last visit here.

Letter 2 (ca. 1133)

[To] Abélard, illustrious master, Abbot of St. Gildas de Rhuys, [from] Héloïse, lowly bride of Christ, in the spirit of abject humility and apology:

Great is the love I have always borne and will ever bear you; believe, my lord, that I have never wished either to hurt or offend you. It grieves me to hear that my last letter did both. I beseech you, humbly, to forgive me for whatever new sorrow my thoughtless words have added to your burden, and pray that your anger towards me be softened. I beg you to believe that it is not that I have been more willing to follow you to hell than to heaven, but that I do not see the way to go that would take me to where you say you are now, which you have so far done nothing to help me see.

At the risk of incurring your further righteous anger, I implore, my lord, that you allow me one final chance to explain myself, before— in true, obedient submission to your will— I silence myself on this subject forever. If it is indeed your will that I play the hypocrite even with you, then it shall be done, though know you, master, that no amount of punishment from God will make me penitent for whatever great sin I supposedly committed in loving you, for I regret nothing. I will repeat often the prayer you wrote for me, begging God to punish me, because you wish me to. But I do not share your faith in the ability of the rod to compel love and true obedience within the innermost recesses of the heart. You know how my uncle would often punish me, calling me willful and stubborn, even after you and I had wed. Never did his punishment move my heart as he intended, and I wonder that you do not remember this when you speak to me of the efficacy of punishment for humbling and opening the human heart. I beg you make plain to me this, master: are you asking me for only blind obedience and commanding me to silence both my heart and my intellect in obeying you?

Everywhere I look I see contradictions I have no means of resolving. You instruct me that love for you should make me long for your death, which alone can free you from a life of unbearable torment, yet say your letter should have consoled me by demonstrating how greatly you deserve my compassion, by which my own complaints are shown to be too petty to be worthy of mention. And yet you say also that I should feel fortunate myself to have felt the punishing hand of God and not even wish for compassion from you or anyone else. Do you not see the contradiction in these three premises?

Moreover, you deride my "gullibility" in having believed any of the "lies" you say you told me simply to achieve the satisfaction of your lust, and assure me that there was no sworn covenant between us, but only an elaborate deception meant to snare me into the sinful toils of your will. Do you not think I could distinguish when your lovers' words were simple fantasies meant to delight us both (if that is what you mean by "lies"), fictions as sweet and playful as the songs you wrote and sang to woo me? I never, for example, believed you would "die from love" as you would often say. Nor did I believe that you truly thought me a goddess revealed in an epiphany of ineffable ecstasy (as was said happened with Anchises, after making love to the goddess, who had disguised herself as a mortal). Until that terrible night on which my uncle worked his vengeance, you kept your portion of the covenant as seriously as I did mine. While it is not given to me to know for certain what was ever in your heart, yet I do believe it is only now that you make of our covenant a lie, so to cast a shadow backwards over what was, as to say it was never real, but only delusion on my part.

You say also that our covenant was wicked and shameful and showed contempt for God. Do you not know, master, that our covenant has always been a law written in my heart, commanding its obedience even when both it and reason move my will otherwise? Both my heart and my intellect told me marriage was wrong, and that it would endanger both you and our love. And both my heart and my intellect told me it would be to do violence to consecrate my life to God when my spirit was neither prepared nor truly willing. Yet in both these things I submitted to your will, for our covenant dictated a higher obedience and will, commanding my heart above all else, whose utmost will and highest intent has always been to fulfill that sacred bond. You order me now to forget it and never to speak of it again. I have thought and thought, seeking understanding of how you could abandon me in this, too, which you always swore to be inviolable. Yet my intellect fails me, leading me to suspect that what the world whispers is correct, that you make this most wretched of nullifications because you do not forgive me for my uncle's vengeance and repudiate every tie and bond between us, denying even that you ever loved me, spurred solely by hatred of me for my uncle's sake.

Know, master, that if you abrogate our covenant you erase, also, the woman I am, making of me a shade of Hades as it were, invisible, soundlessly wailing, soulless, where before I only dwelled in Tartarus, tormented like Tantalus with a hunger and thirst that Fortune had decreed be never more assuaged.

Everything that we have been, one to the other, was made possible only through the bond of our covenant. For love of you, my deity, I vanquished all fear of anything the world could do to hurt me, never caring for any opprobrium but yours. God knows (and probably you do, too) that I would never have shown myself so audacious as to address you as "beloved" (or even by your so dear name) had it not been your command that I do so, just as I would have lacked the boldness to obey your every wish for serving pleasure, so entirely did maidenly shame once rule me.

Yet because a covenant is useless when one side ruptures its sworn bonds; and because I have always sought to please you above all else; even in this my lord, though you once said we would be bound by our covenant through eternity, I, most unhappy and wretched of women ever cursed by Fortune and abandoned by their lovers, submit myself to your will in utmost abjection. It is, henceforth, done.

But the list of my offenses does not end there. You moreover chastise me for debasing myself with "self-pollution" and order me to confess and repent this sin at once to my spiritual director. Can you have forgotten our discussions while you were here, and the passages in the book on women's diseases by Magistra Trotula, advising for the treatment of my woman's disorder massage of my private parts if intercourse with my husband is not possible? Though many men call us the weaker sex for Eve's sin (of which Adam, too, was culpable), you know why truly we are called the weaker sex, such that it is thought perilous to admit women to the religious life before the flowing of their courses has ceased, lest lack of sexual intercourse cause congestion and the many deleterious effects that often result therefrom. For St. Jerome, the great preacher of continence, wrote: "It is my wish, therefore, that young widows shall marry again, have children and preside over a home. Then they will give no opponent occasion for slander." And St. Paul in writing to Timothy rules that "A widow should not be put on the roll under sixty years of age. . . . Avoid younger widows." You say that the proof of my tendency to continence is in my having tried to dissuade you from carnal acts during Lent and on other holy occasions. But surely you must remember that was only the first time, when I still perceived a shame to dwell in carnal acts. And I would also remind you that I am not even as old now as you were at the time we were lovers.

Why do you reprove me? You understood all this when you visited us here. Do you not recollect that when we discussed it and I mentioned that I intended to ask Sister Marie, our infirmarian, to perform the treatment, you reacted with such horror at the thought that you said it would be better that you yourself do it and, speaking of the marriage debt, said that it would be no sin in God's eyes. Your gentle, tender ministrations in the privacy of the poplars, by releasing my seed, for a time restored my weak woman's body to health. Yet when as we rose to our feet and I kissed your kind hands you saw the old serf watching us from where he stood by the mill-wheel, you grew cold and angry and disgusted with my weakness.

I beg you now to take into consideration my weakness and not to blame me for it so harshly. I am young, and my body's cold and wet humors cause my seed to congest. You have repeatedly insisted that it would be inappropriate for my sisters to see my weakness, even our infirmarian Sister Marie, and so I have, obediently, concealed my infirmity. If memories of our passionate embraces are always in my mind, they are there because you directed my heart so. The occasions I remember may be long past, but I am young, and they are all the possessions I own, and most especially the last relics of what you have been to me, however you repudiate me now.

You further instruct me to hate the world and everyone in it for God's sake, and to do good only for love of him. But there is no hate in me, my lord, unless it be for the false apostles and wicked abbots and bishops who call you heretic and seek your ruin. If to love God is to hate you, then it is sure I never can or will, nor would want to.

And finally, you task me with ingratitude for all the husbandly care you have taken for me. Yet never, my lord, did I ask, expect, or desire husbandly concern from you. Do not blame me if I am not properly grateful to you for having paid a dowry to Argenteuil for me, for by your own account you did it not from charity or love, but to satisfy your own notions of honor. Though I at first believed you intended our relationship to continue on a new plane, it became obvious very soon that you wished me to enter holy orders only to be rid of me. And so my situation could not have mattered to me less. I am, however, grateful that you gave me and my sisters shelter here at the Paraclete when we were thrust homeless into the world after Suger took Argenteuil for St. Denis. You told me the last time I saw you when I tried to thank you that you wanted to hear nothing of it, because, you said, you were pleased to know the oratory you built would be given over to constant service to God. If your giving us a home here was an act of husbandly concern, then I humbly acknowledge and thank you for it.

Discretion is the mother of virtue and has been my special province since the day we parted. It has been long since you have sent me word of Astrolabe. You long ago ordered me not to communicate with our son or anyone at Le Pallet, but though I will continue to respect your wishes in most things, in this one particular, since you commanded me to avoid contact, solely (you said) "for my own good," I consider that with the dissolution of our bond you have given me the freedom to do as I will. Fear not, master. You may be sure I will do him no harm nor mention you at all in any letter I write to him.

We envy your students their great good fortune. May God preserve you, master, now that he has delivered you from your most wretched captivity in that Babylon in the wilderness.

Letter 3 (ca. 1134)

[To] her master, or rather her father, her husband, or rather brother; [from] his handmaid, or rather his daughter, wife, or rather sister; to Abélard, Héloïse:

We read your Easter sermon yesterday, and both my sisters and our guests listened intently, even the Lady Jeanne, whom Count Theobald two weeks past brought to sojourn with us through Easter. Though the text of your sermon is an exemplar of lucidity to the eye of she who perceives it directly from the page, since to the bodily ear of even the most attentive listeners long, elegant sentences such as you, master, write so beautifully and excellently, can nevertheless be difficult to follow, we amended it for greater clarity and ease of comprehension.

We also sang the Nocturne you sent us for Good Friday. Our Chantress especially owes grateful thanks that with your assistance we are able to put our house into better order, while I myself am in particular grateful that whenever this lady of uncertain relation to Count Theobald hums, in my presence, one of the songs you wrote for me in our earlier life, I can recommend to her your more recent works as not only worthy of her attention, but more appropriate here at the Paraclete.

A matter of tremendous importance, master, demands that we seek your most sage advice and guidance. If my script seems less firm to you than it should, it is not a reflection of illness or weakness in body or spirit, but rather of the turmoil into which we here have been lately precipitated. I should perhaps not have hesitated so long before sending to you, but lacked the words (as I still do) to describe what has happened. Moreover, I possessed no time during Holy Week to allow me to attempt to do so, and even if I had chosen to steal the time from my duties it yet seemed improper to send our messenger out onto the road until after we had finished celebrating Easter.

Reason, my lord, dictates that we be wary of naming this or that thing as a miracle or a special, privileged, manifestation from God. We have often seen that people delude themselves and sometimes deliberately delude others as to appearances which might on first sight seem to have flown from God. Yet even as I write, perched on my stool at my desk in the library, I am forced to take notice of what my own and my sisters' eyes cannot help but see. Since the Wednesday of Holy Week, there has appeared, on the stand before me (on which I ordinarily position whatever book I am studying or copying), the image— composed, it would seem, entirely of light— of an opened scroll lying flat against the wood, and beside my stand a pile of some three dozen other scrolls. Yet when I stretch out my hand to touch it, it meets nothing but air, and then the solid wood of the stand— though what I see is the scroll superimposed over my own flesh. The script on the scroll, though strangely formed and full of abbreviations unfamiliar to me, is clearly Greek. I believe that I could probably read much of what is written on this opened scroll made only of light. I know, for example, that the title at the top reads "The Secret Book of Saint John."

Lest you think I am hallucinating (as I myself feared when the scrolls first appeared on my desk), know you that the library had more occupants than usual, sisters urged there by me to read the texts the Rule recommends for all who are literate to study and meditate upon during Holy Week. And consequently, most of my sisters have seen this apparition, too. As far as we know, it has been present on my desk, without ceasing, since last Wednesday morning. The sight of it is most fearful and fills all of us with great anxiety and dread. And so I have thus far read only the title. Please, wise master and kind father, advise us on what we should do. I have ordered everyone who has seen it to silence, and have even forbidden discussion of this apparition among ourselves, lest any guest or servant hear of it and spread report of it abroad. Though the sight is dreadful, my inclination is to think that God has for some reason favored me, who knows Greek, with this special visitation. While Satan is known to perpetrate devilish hoaxes on poor, wretched men and women, it is hard for me to understand with what evil he could here be tempting me, since my particular weakness must be apparent and exposed for him to see.

We beseech you, my lord, to reply without delay. We do not know how long it can be before word of this apparition becomes public. Your counsel would be most welcome in preparing us for that eventuality.

Farewell. And may God keep you safe, and grant all good speed to your answer.

Letter 4 (ca. 1134)

[To] her master, father, husband, and brother, Abélard; [from] his handmaid, daughter, wife, and sister, Héloïse:

It seems best to write you again, although my man has not yet returned from taking you the last letter. You will find enclosed a portion of Greek text, which is a copy of the page I made from the apparition that continues to appear on my desk. If the letters are not as perfectly formed as they ought to be, this is because the copy I am sending you was made by my pupil Denise. I lacked the time myself to write out a second copy; and I believe the letters are formed clearly, if not masterfully.

Not long after I sent my messenger speeding to you, I began to reconsider my deep reluctance to examine the apparitional text with closer scrutiny. I realized that my fear and dread of it arose because of the ghostliness of its appearance rather than any profound conviction I had of its evil. We know that God has often, from Old Testament times forward, manifested himself and signs of himself through light. Satan, on the contrary, usually works through more material means. My fear, I concluded, was the general fear of the supernatural rather than of evil. It then became clear to my intellect that my fear, while not groundless, was base. And so I resolved to overcome it. I went to my desk and copied out the page that there appeared, then carefully checked my work, letter by letter, to be certain I had copied it correctly. I then asked one of the pupils to whom I have been teaching Greek to make, as carefully as she could, a copy from my copy. When I returned to my desk, thinking to study the ghostly page I had just copied, I discovered it had changed to a new page which I believe to be a continuation of that I had just copied. My heart almost stopped when I saw it, as when I first beheld the apparition on my desk last Wednesday of Holy Week.

My lord, it seems to me a sign that I must copy out the pages as they appear. I will do this and will direct Denise to make copies from my copies, and in the meantime set myself to translate the Greek into Latin. Since your Greek comes so much more slowly than mine, I write here my translation of the first few sentences:

> It happened one day that John, the brother of James (who are the sons of Zebedee), went up to the temple. There Amanaias, a Pharisee, approached him and said unto him: "Where is your master whom you followed?" And John said unto him, "He has returned to the place from which he came." And the Pharisee said: "This Nazarene deceived and misled you, and hardened your hearts and estranged you from your fathers' tradition."

Unless you send me instruction to cease copying and translating this text, I will continue to work with it. I have no idea what else to do. My sisters have grown so excited that it has become difficult to prevent their discussing it among themselves. The only example of such an occurrence any of us have been able to think of is the case of Daniel. At Belshazzar's feast, the fingers of a man's hand wrote on the wall of the king's palace, and Daniel was brought before the king to interpret it. But they were only four words, Mene, Mene, Tekel, Upharsin, by which Daniel prophesied that Belshazzar's kingdom would be divided and taken by the Medes and Persians. Yet these words are many, and they are replaced with new words after they have been copied.

Never have we needed your guidance so much as now. We implore you to send us your wise counsel without delay. Farewell.

Letter 5 (ca. 1134)

[To] her master, father, brother, and husband, Abélard, [from] his handmaid, daughter, wife, and sister, Héloïse:

I am writing this now to have ready when my first messenger returns with your reply so that I may send it off to you with all possible haste. I have copied many and many pages of the first Greek text, as well as of a second which has followed it. What I have translated troubles me deeply. I so fear, master, that it savors of heresy, such that a great dread overtakes me whenever I settle to work at my desk. Should we perhaps be avoiding the library altogether? Should we send to the bishop, that he be brought here to perform an exorcism of it? This question weighs heavily on my heart. I have prayed to God that he might help me find the answer, and I have also brought Father Louis into our confidence and shown him the apparition. But he is as troubled and uncertain as I as to the nature of this vision or how we should proceed with respect to it. His only suggestion is to notify you, and possibly the bishop. It has now been two weeks since it first began to appear to us. Can it be possible that Satan has such great power as to be capable of sustaining this strange apparition so constantly, and for so long? But even if he does, to what evil could he hope to tempt us, and why in this way, through a vision of words that manifest themselves in a shower of never-dimming radiance?

My lord, I take up my pen again where I left off writing two days past. Another manifestation of Light has come upon us, in addition to the one that still burns on my desk, and so I will finish this letter and send it off tomorrow by yet another man, whether my first messenger has returned or not. (It is a great extravagance, but the matter has become too urgent to allow for delay.) The new manifestation of Light has come to us in the oratory, over the altar. It burst forth while we were at mass this morning, during the Gloria, in a sudden shower of white so brilliant it at first blinded us and caused Father Louis great difficulty in continuing. When little by little our sight returned, the Light remained, above the altar, shedding such great intensity that even the darkest corner of the chapel was clearly visible, making it necessary for us to keep our eyes averted from the altar, since looking directly at it would surely be as painful and injurious to them as staring into the sun.

Surely the Light must come from God, who we must assume will bestow upon us the understanding necessary for knowing the reason for its appearance. Yet my fears that the words that continue to be revealed in the library, which are so difficult to understand, may be heretical, do not abate. The text, as far as I can read it, speaks often of Light, though confusingly. If I am translating correctly, one passage in the text, for example, reads: "The fount of the Spirit flowed from the living river of light. And it furnished all Aeons and all worlds in every way. It understood its own image, when it saw it in the pure river of light which surrounds it." I have never, master, felt so stupid, as I do when regarding this text and trying to grasp its meaning.

It is not your wish, you have told me, to come here to the Paraclete while you yet live. But I fear that if you do not come to us now, we must beg the bishop's counsel and guidance. If the bishop decides that the Light is not of God, can you doubt he would order us to leave here and go elsewhere on the assumption that staying here we risk contamination by an evil more powerful than has ever been known to inhabit a place dedicated to performing Divine Office?

It is for you, our founder, to decide. Farewell.

Letter 6 (ca. 1134)

[To] her most beloved husband and brother in Christ, [from] his wife and sister in Christ:

Your departure four days ago left us saddened, yet filled with the bliss of having seen you again, in the body and alive, as we had nevermore hoped to do. When the portress sent to tell us of your arrival at our gate, my heart filled with such joy as to nearly burst out of my body, through my chest. It is true that I had forgotten, when thinking of you (for the oldest memories remain, in my mind, the most potent), to remind myself that age and sorrow and illness have been in all the years of absence steadily leaving their mark on your person. Yet in the traces of care and past injuries scoring your face and tormenting your body, your greatness becomes all the more apparent, and the erectness of your figure that much more impressive. Your coldness, in seldom allowing our eyes to meet, I dare to hope came not from displeasure with me, for your words of praise, though unwarranted, seemed to argue otherwise.

Yet I wish, my lord, that you had allowed us to speak in private, so that I could make clear to you why it is incorrect to presume that God has marked me for a specially holy task and favor. Still, your very presence as well as the wise counsel you offered us acted upon me as both elixir and balm, lifting my weary spirit in exultation and calming my troubled and fearful heart. I have accordingly been striving to achieve that state of mind and soul to which you urged me, to ready myself for whatever task it is God has chosen to put on me. You say it can be no accident that he chose the desk of one of the few in Latin Christendom who in our day have been taught the rudiments of Greek; and that the altar of the oratory you built to the Paraclete, though rude and humble in comparison with the ostentatious wealth of the great abbeys and cathedrals, is as worthy, and perhaps worthier than any other site dedicated to God's worship. Such reasoning makes sense to me. Yet how can I fail to doubt that our entire personal history was intended by God to lead me here to the Paraclete, so as to be at this place, ready to receive whatever new revelation and prophesy it is his will to hand down to his creatures? My life has never been marked by any special signs of grace, such as has often been observed of people marked by God for his especial purposes. Though, to please you, I have adopted a chaste life outwardly obedient to the tenets of our rule, I have never felt close to God, and even now, though you say I have been chosen for a special task, feel only bewilderment, confusion, and dread (which your powerful sermon, master, has greatly eased though not erased). You must have known I could not dispute with you before my sisters nor make it plain to you just how unfit I am to serve as you described. Only you, dear master, know how impossible it is that God would choose me as a recipient for singular favor; to you only have I confessed that it is you I seek to please, and not God.

The bishop's clerk, by name Guillaume, arrived last night, to visit us in the bishop's stead as he told you he would do when you went to Troyes to consult with him. As you advised, we took our visitor to the oratory first, to see how brilliantly the cross above the altar is now illumined. This clerk Guillaume prostrated himself for some time, and when he arose to his feet was shown to be as violently trembling as the leaves on the poplars visible from the dormitory windows. We next led him into the library, to my desk. On seeing the radiant text and piles of scrolls, the man fell to his knees and mumbled a long, hoarse prayer to God, thanking him for sending us this "miracle," and asking that we be made worthy of it. I then showed him the large sheaf of pages we had so far copied, but of course, being without Greek, he could only stare at the texts without comprehension. Yes, yes, he constantly repeated, this is a wonderful sign of favor with which God has blessed us. Clearly God wishes us to study these texts he has seen fit to reveal to us.

The long and the short of it is, Guillaume approves, in the bishop's name, our accepting assistance from the scholar you have recommended be brought here from Cluny. Yet I own deep reservations to these presumptions that the Light and texts are blessings and revelations come to us from God. I have been working diligently on the translation of one text in particular because its syntax is so simple and repetitive (in the form, I believe, of a hymn) that it is not so taxing and frustrating to my humblingly limited abilities. It begins promisingly enough "I was sent forth from Power, to appear among those who contemplate me. . ." almost persuading me its purport would be an explanation for these manifestations of radiant Light. But after a prologue, most of the body of the text issues in the form of "I am this, but also that"— the "this" and "that" being in each instance in opposition to one another. Thus, "I am the whore and the saint, I am the mother and the girl child, I am the womb and the barren one of whom her sons are many." Surely these texts must all be allegories and parables, and consequently difficult of understanding. It is said that God works in mysterious ways, and that there are mysteries of his Truth that it is not given to us on this earth to know. But surely those like the Abbot of Clairveaux who often and vigorously invoke the mysteriousness of God's Truth and purposes do so only to stifle the use of reason for fathoming and interpreting them, which they say leads to heresy.

And finally, my lord, I fear that now this Guillaume has seen the Light, we will soon be inundated with visitors eager to see it with their own eyes, and also to judge its meaning. He has declared it a "holy manifestation." I doubt we will be allowed any peace in carrying out our duties as long as it persists.

We continue here to copy the pages of text as they appear on my desk, and I to work at translating them and in meditation and prayer as you advised. Though I cannot share your faith in the wisdom of any legate his holiness sends (for, without accusing the pope's own representative of calumny, I cannot forget how Mathew of Albano accepted the unfounded allegation of Argenteuil's "infamy" without question, to please the abbot who lusted after its wealth), I know that your advice that we request such a visitation is wise.

I own, dear master, reservations, too, at having any men here besides you working in our library (and so humble a place by comparison with Cluny's magnificence). God forbid that all these men culminate in driving my sisters and me from our home and work as was done to us previously. Though they don't speak of it, I can both see in the faces and hear in the voices of those sisters who came here with me from Argenteuil their fear that this second home, like that first one, will become again to us as the Garden became to Adam and Eve after the Fall. I have reminded them of the charter Innocent himself has granted us, but the lesson of Argenteuil has taught our hearts to doubt. Where value is seen to lie, the powerful do as they will.

Your handmaids pray that the exertions of your journey will not have exhausted all your strength and strained your delicate health. God knows that we would have preferred you to stay here an extra day after your trip to Troyes, before returning to Paris, both for your sake and for ours. Know you, dear master, that we are grateful for all your paternal attention and counsel. Do not desert us when we need your wisdom most. Know you that we place utmost faith in your guidance through whatever trials lie ahead. Farewell.

Letter 7 (ca. 1134)

[To] Abélard, her wise master, Héloïse his handmaid and wife:

I have just received your letter and have asked your man to stay an extra night so that I may write a reply for him to carry back to you. The Paraclete, dear master, has since I last wrote you been favored with many visitors. Not only have lay lords and ladies come here to see the Light in the oratory, but we have even been honored by a visit from Peter, the reverend Abbot of Cluny, and all his retinue with him (which must be nearly as grand as the King's). Our cellaress, Sister Margaret, felt great distress at not being able to provide him with such excellent food and wine as that to which he is accustomed. But I believe that the reverend abbot approved our humble arrangements, for when he spoke to us in Chapter he lavished on us his approbation for the excellence of our performance of the Office, and refrained from making any disapproving comment on our use of "supersubstantial" instead of "daily" in the Our Father. And like our other visitors, he made us a generous gift before departing. But I am troubled (though under his high gaze of approval I often found myself swelling with exultation) to report that he spoke at some length about my "great erudition," which he said he had admired even before I chose to put it to "holy" uses only, and about how God had clearly chosen me for "some great task" because of it, and about my "great piety" for which, he said, I was "justly famed." Never has my merely outward profession felt so false and wicked. I could not look into his eyes when he spoke thus, and could feel the blood stinging my cheeks. At which he chided me gently for resisting acknowledgment of what God had "made plain."

The venerable Peter, no doubt for the most charitable and honorable of reasons, increased my embarrassment by persistently calling me "sister" and titling me "abbess" (which my other visitors as well as my sisters soon began to mimic). At my look of startlement, he spared me the shame of attempting to correct my superior by saying that it had been decided that the Paraclete was to be named a monastery and I its abbess, and that Pope Innocent would in due course be inscribing a charter to that effect. I did not inquire as to what he meant by the words "it has been decided." It would please me to see the Paraclete given such official recognition (though the Pope's recent charter to me already promises protection of our possession of it); but I know that even such a powerful charter as that would not necessarily stand up if, should the winds shift, they blow strongly enough. There is also the not inconsiderable factor of my age, which is (as you have yourself noted) unsuitable for the position (though my duties have from the beginning here been that of abbess).

God knows I have never wished any attention paid to the Paraclete except by you, cherished master. Still, we have been grateful for the bounty of gifts the generosity of others have bestowed on us, for our lives would be miserable here indeed without them. (When I think of how dear parchment alone is!)

I am grateful, master, for your attention in your letter to what you call my "doubts." You liken these manifestations of Light to that which struck the apostle on the road to Damascas. But how can I presume to think God would care so much to single out me? You urge me to open my heart to loving him (and forsaking all my "old delusions"), and to trusting that he will show me the way. Dearest master, you do not know how difficult it now is for me even to enter the oratory and to sing my part when we chant the Offices. Nor do the sight of those unearthly pages on my desk ever fail to make my stomach churn. These manifestations of Light make me feel nothing but anxiety, either because I do not recognize their meaning, or because I am miserably aware of my unworthiness. Yet I will continue to heed your counsel (when, that is, the flow of visitors allows me the time for prayer and meditation).

I send you additional pages of the texts and a copy of the translations that I and Brother Étienne from Cluny have so far essayed, and hope that this finds you in good health. Farewell, my only love.

Letter 8 (ca. 1134)

[To] her reverend master, Abélard, his dutiful handmaid, Héloïse:

Everything you say that you have heard about the Paraclete from the Bishop of Paris is true. We have been overwhelmed with pilgrims, not stopping the night on their way to a shrine, but coming to the Paraclete itself, as though it were itself a shrine. If our oratory were a great cathedral, or our house a great abbey, this would create no difficulty. But we can neither house all these guests, nor crowd such multitudes of worshipers into the oratory. Indeed, there are more people here than at the warm fair,[8] now being held at Troyes. And so they are indeed camped outside our gate, begging admission. As for the stories about miracles, a number of people claimed to have been healed "in the Light of the Paraclete" (as they call it), and two of my sisters and three of our young boarders have been "struck with the Light" and converted. (Perhaps you could be tempted, my lord, to celebrate mass in the Light? Would it not be a miracle worthy of the Paraclete, if it were to make its founder whole again?) Coin and other contributions are flowing into our coffers at a most astonishing rate, but we have had to make enormous purchases of wheat, legumes, and other victuals in order to feed the great numbers that have come. Too, visits from knights and nobility never cease, whether from curiosity, or from the desire to "be washed in the Light." I strive to continue our mission, but doing so grows increasingly difficult.

As a consequence I myself have never a moment of peace and no time for working on the Greek texts. The refuge of the Paraclete, given our mission of devotion, study, and contemplation, has been overrun by the world. Does God not, indeed, work in mysterious ways?

You, reverend master, possessing far greater wisdom than this very weak female, will know best whether she deserves to be chastised for not having kept the Paraclete's founder informed of what has happened here. She wishes only to remind him that she was instructed not to burden and ensnare him with unnecessary communication.

[8] 12th-century Troyes held two annual fairs, attracting merchants from all over France and Flanders. One, held in June, was called the "warm fair," the other, in October, called the "cold fair."

Letter 9 (ca. 1134)

[To] Abélard, her wise master, Héloïse, bride of Christ:

The pages enclosed contain a new translation of the text that first appeared on my desk, called "The Secret Book of Saint John," which you specifically requested that I ask Brother Étienne from Cluny to undertake, so that it could be compared with the translation I made earlier. When Brother Étienne finished his translation, he and I went over our two versions carefully, sentence by sentence, to compare and discuss. Although there are many small differences, in only five places did we diverge substantially in our interpretation (which greatly relieved my mind, since the subject of the text is so difficult of understanding).

You are better qualified to judge the text than either Brother Étienne or I. But it seems to us both that it is heretical. Although much of it is unintelligible to us, it states clearly, for one thing, that God himself had a mother, who made him imperfectly, because she made him by herself, without her consort. And that he (i.e., God), called "the arrogant one," in turn displeased his mother by stealing power from her, in order to create the cosmos. And the text proclaims that God's statement that he is a jealous God, "by announcing this, indicated to the angels that another God exists," arguing that God could not be jealous if there were not another God to be jealous of. And it also tells an entirely different version of the Fall, calling Eve "Epinoia," saying that she appeared <u>as a light</u> and awakened their reasoning, and gives an equally blasphemous version of the Great Flood.

Everywhere, throughout the text, are references to light, my lord. Epinoia, or Eve, is characterized as "luminous." Even if the text is meant metaphorically, I don't see how it can be anything other than heretical. Since light is at the heart of the text, and it is light that floods the altar in the oratory and brings materially insubstantial texts to my desk, they surely must be connected.

Brother Étienne says that your knowledge of the holy Doctors surpasses his. You will know, he says, which of the Doctors excoriated such ideas, which he believes were once rampant and a serious threat to the Church.

Farewell.

Letter 10 (ca. 1134)

[To] her reverend master, Abélard, [from] Héloïse, in humble obedience:

I write to you on the heels of your departure, as it were, only because I must. Would that you had remained twenty-four hours longer! Last night, or rather early this morning, well before Matins,[9] I awoke with a very strong will to leave my bed and go down to the library. You know that I have always faithfully and strictly enforced the rule that no sister may leave the dormitory in the night except to perform the Office, unless she has my permission and is escorted by another sister. Having always been careful to enforce the rule, I strove mightily to resist this urge, but it proved too powerful for me to withstand. It was as though a voice spoke in my mind, driving me out of the dormitory, drawing me inexorably to the library. Such was my haste that I rose in my shift, putting on neither shoes, robe, nor veil.

Since it was a very fine, clear night, bright with the light of the midsummer moon and stars, I did not stop to take one of the lights we keep burning through the night, but hurried as quickly as I could down the treacherous stairs, into the cloister. The night was still and quiet, except for the harsh chitter of summer insects. My heart pounded violently with trepidation as I faced the door into the library. The very thought of beholding that unearthly light on my desk, glowing unnaturally

[9] Matins was generally sung between 2:30 and 3:00 a.m.

in the dark, made me fearful and hesitant. The Light in the oratory, my lord, has never seemed so unnatural or dreadful as the radiant texts on my desk. But the impulse to enter the library could not be resisted. And lo, entering, I found that chamber filled with a column of Light rising before my desk, brilliant enough to illumine most of the room, though not so powerfully as its manifestation in the oratory. I felt within me the call to go to my desk, to the Light, though my body trembled violently, and though the desire to fall to my knees in dread-filled awe pressed me most urgently. In that moment I knew in my heart that the Light had called me, and for the first time believed that you had been right in saying that I had been specially chosen for some Task. Although I was frightened, I could feel in all of my body and heart and soul that this call was holy, and no trickery of Satan. For I was overwhelmed with even more powerful feelings than any you have inspired in me, with feelings that made me want to cry out, or sing, and beat my breast in expression of them. Yet from a place deep within I knew that I must hold myself still, in readiness to listen and receive instruction for whatever Task I had been chosen.

As I approached, my sight adjusted a little to the Light, and I grew less blinded, so that I found I could look into it (as it is not possible to do with the Light in the oratory). The lineaments of a Being looked out at me. His body, I could see, was clad in a tunic like pink-veined marble, his calves and feet were naked, and a helmet or crown covered all of his head but his face. A great voice whose rich timbre seemed to throb all around me addressed me "Blessed, learned Héloïse."[10] I sank to my knees at his feet, but he bade me sit on my stool behind my desk on the dais. And so with much trembling I obeyed, and seated myself as he had said.

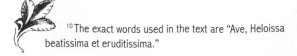

[10] The exact words used in the text are "Ave, Heloissa beatissima et eruditissima."

What followed would take many and many pages of writing to tell. The angel (for so I think of him, though he said he was not among the ranks of what we think of as angels, that he was not like Gabriel or Michael, but above them) bade me afterwards to write down everything I can recall of what he said to me, this time as well as all the other times to come in which he will visit me. This I have begun to do, but there is so much, that I decided that I must write to you at once, rather than wait to send you a fuller report, which will take me several days, I believe, to produce.

My lord, the reproaches you delivered to me during the visit you just ended here still scald me with shame. It pains me intolerably that you think me prideful and vain and petulant. And yet I must add one more thing. I have told only Sister Marie about the visitation (for she it was who discovered me in the library, when Matins rang and I was not found in my bed) and have asked her not to speak of it to anyone until I have first received guidance from you. But despite that, great attention is now being drawn to me because, since the visitation, there has been visible around my head (or so the sisters and Father Louis say) an aura of Light, faint but evident even in the brightest of daylight. And so you may understand, my lord, why your obedient handmaid is especially grateful, or rather joyful that during your visit here you arranged to relieve her of enough of her duties that she may return to her study and meditations.

Farewell.

Letter 11 (ca. 1334)

[To] her reverend master, Abélard, Héloïse, in loving obedience:

[11] Literally, the feminine form of the word *messenger*, which we have chosen to keep in Latin, since Héloïse uses the word as a name (while we have rendered such names as Héloïse, Abélard, Marie into French versions because doing so involves transliteration, not translation).

Nuntia,[11] as the angel (who is not truly an angel) bade me address him (or should I say her, since the name is feminine though the Being appears to be masculine), called me for the second night to the library, again before Matins. "Hail, Héloïse," he said (again calling me blessed and learned). And then he asked me why I had not spoken to the sisters in Chapter about all that he had said to me in the night. Because he spoke sternly, I trembled in fear that he might be angry with me. "I did not know that was your will," I answered (as shakily as I used to do when you first began to teach me at my uncle's). "Do you not trust me," Nuntia responded, "that you must seek your husband's guidance before teaching others what I have taught you? Did Moses consult first with his wife before handing down the commandments to his people?"

I hardly knew what to say. Tell me, most learned master, did Moses even have a wife? This question buzzed in my head, like a gnat distracting me, as Nuntia continued chiding me for what he said was my "too great dependence" on your direction. Dread-stricken, I admitted that I was unworthy and that although I was willing to be his handmaid, many others would be worthier. This exasperated Nuntia; yet he ceased to berate me and told me we would resume our lesson where we had left off when Matins rang the night before.

Forgive me, master, for because Nuntia reproved me, I this day spoke in Chapter to the sisters about the revelations he has made to me, though during your last visit here I promised not to speak to anyone without first consulting you should it happen that I be honored with divine revelation. I cannot hope to write everything that he said to me on both nights, but I will try to convey to you the principal points.

First, let me say that Nuntia's Latin is peculiar. It is without grammatical error, yet is somehow strange, as is the rhythm of his speech. This sometimes distracted me, as did the radiance that always surrounds him and the recurrence of fear that again and again washes over me in his presence, as the occasional gust of wind ruffles the poplars on a fine summer's day.

Nuntia began first with a parable. Consider, he said, the mother who suckles her child with the milk of her breast. In infancy, the child, so fed, thrives, for without teeth and a mature digestion, the child cannot absorb alimentation any other way, and the milk contains every nutriment necessary for his good health. This same mother swaddles her infant's limbs, to prevent him from harm, and to ensure that his limbs grow straight. But as the infant matures, the mother begins to feed the child solid food and unbinds his limbs so that he can learn to crawl, and then walk, and finally run. She does not keep him bound in cloths, in his cradle, for all of his life, nor does she suckle him into manhood. Nor does she slap her child when he learns any word other than "Mama."

Yet a mother, named Ecclesia,[12] has done just that. Ecclesia has restricted the diet of her children to breast milk and has kept her children in swaddling clothes and not allowed them out of their cradles, and has refused to allow her children to learn speech except for the one word she wants to hear them say, "Mama." For centuries she has taken the children God has given her and stunted their growth and silenced them into ignorance and doltishness. God has watched, greatly sorrowed at the stupidity and jealousness of Ecclesia's love. But

[12] *Ecclesia* is Latin for "Church."

God will watch, Nuntia announced, no longer. For it is not true that what happens in this world is unimportant because the next world, so much better, is yet to come. God would not have allowed the Earth to have come into existence if that were so. And God can see that if Ecclesia continues as before, the Earth will grow more miserable and wicked, and terrible injustices will be perpetrated against God's children, more than at any time in the millennium.

"You, Héloïse, will bring Enlightenment to Christendom," Nuntia told me. "You, Héloïse, have been chosen to begin the great Transformation that will reform all of Europe." These words I tell you verbatim, wise master, for they are burned into my mind as though a brand had set them forever into my flesh. He spoke at length about the early Church, and hinted at the future. Among the many things he told me, he said that it would shortly be decided to press the pope to recognize the Paraclete as a monastery with me named its abbess, and that he knew the pope would grant that and other favors in order to consolidate his support in the face of the schism that continues to challenge his authority. Is this true, my lord? That the pope's support from bishops and archbishops and abbots and the lay nobility is in exchange for favors even at this moment being specified to him?

And Nuntia said also that on the first of August in the 1137th year of our Lord, Louis the king would die, and that six months later the antipope would die also, and because Innocent then would no longer need the support of the whole Frankish clergy, and because with the king's death Bernard of Cîteaux would be very powerful, that if nothing were done to stop him, you, dearest master, would be condemned as a heretic at a mockery of a council to be held at Sens. What must we do to stop Bernard? I implored Nuntia to tell me, terrified at the doom he predicts. But he calmed me, saying that we had six years in which to work against such an outcome. And when I asked him why he could not simply prevent such a thing from happening if it were God's will that it not be so, he chided me for thinking the cosmos so simple as to be tampered with idly, without regard for consequences.

Believe me, my lord, it is no false modesty when I say that I lack understanding and believe that the task Nuntia has set me is beyond both my comprehension and abilities, and even my character. When I reminded him that the apostle had said that women are not to teach, he said that a copyist had inserted that and similar passages into the manuscripts in order to put those words into the apostle's mouth. He said that in the earliest years of the Church there had been many women priests and bishops, but that later, Ecclesia had banned women from teaching and corrupted Paul's texts and declared anyone advocating the ordination of women heretical. And then he reminded me that *ekklesia*, in the Greek, first signified the Athenian assembly of free males, and later, the gathering of people met to celebrate the teachings and life of Christ. He said *Ecclesia* has strayed far from its origins as *ekklesia*. And that it had most often been the case that women, in the early Church, led men into Christian life, rather than vice versa.

Dearest master, I tremble to write such things, even to you. Yet how can I not follow Nuntia's instruction? I know in my heart he has been sent here by God: a powerful purity diffuses from his presence, and there is nothing in any way evil or Satanic about him. Yet everything he has said is anathema. Has Holy Mother Church stunted and starved her children? Any prelate would have me up before an ecclesiastical court on charges of heresy if they heard me saying so: yet I write the words to you, as I relayed them— at Nuntia's insistence— to my sisters today in Chapter.

Nuntia demands that I trust him. He even taught me a short prayer to say, which will call him to me at any time, if not immediately, then as soon as he is free of other concerns that might be occupying him. Although everything he says is strange, when I am in his presence it feels right, within. Yet when I am again alone, it is as though a great all-encompassing warmth has been withdrawn, leaving me aware of how thin my cloak is, how savage the wind.

I beseech you not to be wroth with me, but to advise me as to what I should do. Nuntia describes you as one who has learned to struggle against the swaddling cloths with which Ecclesia bound your limbs, and who has learned a few more words than "Mama," though it has won you only the blows of her chastisement. Do not be angry, most beloved master, when I tell you that Nuntia has said he would talk to you, too, if you were to come here to the Paraclete. I only pass on his words because he bade me do so, not to ensnare you.

Farewell.

Letter 12 (ca. 1334)

[To] her beloved master and reverend lord, Abélard, Héloïse in joyful humility:

Yesterday Nuntia appeared to us all in Chapter and announced that it was his wish that the sisters take instruction from him outside the gate on the banks of the Ardusson, following Compline. And so heeding his command, we went after the service in a group to the gate and with great reluctance passed out into the press of people who have pitched camp there, through which we had need of walking in order to reach the place Nuntia had named. As we passed, people fell to their knees when they saw the aura it is said continues to glow around my head, and calling me "Heloissa Beatissima," begged me to touch them with my grace. Their adoration filled me with as much dread in my loins as the appearance of the texts of Light on my desk, or the sound of your feet on the stairs in my uncle's house. Although I wished to tell them they must not think I have a healing touch, I kept silent, as Nuntia's voice, very quietly in my ear, bade me (though his form was not near me). Some few dozen women from the camp followed us at a distance, which Nuntia permitted, and knelt in the grass a little way off from us when we sisters sat, at Nuntia's instruction, in a circle around him. Like the moon when risen in the dazzling, heavenly firmament of day, the Light surrounding him was not so bright in the lingering rays of the sun, which had begun to lower itself in the sky, but was softer, more beautiful, and delicately tinted (as cannot be seen at night, except with regard to his tunic, which greatly resembles marble). And in this softer light I could see that his helmet or crown was made of a fine mesh of gold and silver strands that stood out from his head in a perfectly even, bright corona.

Nuntia began by saying he wished to talk to us today about God. As always, he spoke only in his strangely stilted Latin. The least learned of my sisters could not have understood everything he said. And the women from camp, nothing, though their faces, when I looked on them, glowed with rapture. He began with a preface on how people who called themselves Christians had closed their ears to the most important things that God had said when he had walked the earth a millennium and a century ago. Open your ears and hearts, he told us, and listen with the full effort of your intellects. Did the Christ not tell you to love your neighbor as yourself? But can it be said that those who call themselves Christians have paid heed to his words?

"Does loving your neighbor as yourself mean killing and persecuting Jews for not sharing your faith? Does loving your neighbor as yourself mean the invasion of warriors into the lands men call 'Holy', to kill and rape and steal from the inhabitants already there? Does loving your neighbor as yourself mean doing what was done to the last great philosopher, Hypatia, in the city of Alexandria four hundred and twelve years after the Christ lived, namely dragging her into a Christian church, stripping her naked and scraping the flesh from her bones with shells, only to quarter her remains and burn them? Does loving your neighbor as yourself mean fighting or sanctioning the fighting of wars, one lord against another? Does loving your neighbor as yourself mean laying siege to the inhabitants of a castle until they surrender from starvation? Does it mean burning villages when their inhabitants refuse to pay the tithe their secular or ecclesiastical lord has levied on them?

"The Lord your God, who is your Father and Mother above, sorrows and grieves that men and women pay so little heed to divine revelation. The laws of the Old Testament were set aside by the Christ; how can the few new laws he laid on you have been so onerous as to have made you forget them?"

Nuntia paused here and looked at us. Behind us, among the common women who had followed us, a baby whimpered. I turned to make a sign to Sister Denise, that the child should be taken some way off, out of the hearing of Nuntia, but Nuntia saw and stopped me. "Let them stay," he said. "For children are a part of God's creation and must be cherished." And then he looked very narrowly at me and said: "Heloissa Beatissima." And questioned me: "Why is it that men kill men, in contempt of the Christ's admonition that they love their neighbor as themselves?"

Though it seemed Nuntia was angry, I felt no hesitation in answering straightly: "Because of original sin, my lord. Original sin makes us all wicked, which is why we need the grace of the sacraments he has so benevolently vouchsafed us."

But Nuntia shook his head. "Original sin was invented by men, centuries after Christ's death. It has been used as a pretext for turning your hearts and minds from the truth, which is that God wishes you to love one another, not wallow in hatred, as you persist in doing."

My heart beat so hard and fast, and my breath came with such constraint, that I feared I would fall ill. The wind rustled through the poplars, ruffling the glassy surface of the river below. Beside me, I could feel Sister Marie trembling.

"We are only women, my lord," Sister Cecile said plaintively. "These things you rebuke us for are the work and concerns of men."

Nuntia gestured to us. "We will not speak of that now," he said. "I have brought you here today to talk of God. I wanted only to alert you to my wish that you open your hearts and minds and remember what I say to you." From the raggedness of their breathing, I knew that my sisters must be distressed as I. "Know you this," Nuntia thundered, as he had not done before, and his single voice was as loud as the sound of the choir chanting in the abbey of St. Denis. "God is not male, as human males are. God is not only your Father. God is both Father and Mother, male and female; in God are to be found both masculine and feminine. When God created human beings, he and she made them in his and her image, male and female. And when God told humans that they were to strive to imitate God, she and he meant not that they were to imitate God's male characteristics only, but all of God's characteristics, both male and female, which are equally divine, neither one superior nor inferior to the other. The major characteristics of God are that he and she created the world and loves the world she and he created. If you would be like God, you too would continue to create the world and love that world you create. You would not despise what you scorn as the flesh, nor would you lay slaughter to one another as you do now. It is said, God is love. If you would be like God, then you would open your hearts to love."

Nuntia's sermon continued a considerable way along this theme. (I am writing fuller notes, which I will later send you, when I have completed the ones I have made from my private lessons with him.) When the light began to fade, he led us in a prayer in which we praised God for loving us and asked him to open our hearts to love, and then we started back for the cloister. Lo, when we turned our eyes from the river, we found at least a hundred people seated behind us, in a great arc. And the joy that leaped in my heart when I saw them was such that I broke into your hymn for Easter, and the sisters joined me, and the others hummed along with us as we returned to the gate.

In the dormitory, several of the sisters wept with joy, fear, and confusion. Some of them, little used to hearing sermons in Latin, were uncertain they had correctly understood Nuntia's speech. Their questions flew fast and thick to me; knowing their need, I answered as best I could and then bade everyone, since night had fallen, to try to sleep. Just before I slipped into the arms of Morphius, wise master, Nuntia spoke again quietly into my ear and told me that I must preach to the people who had gathered outside the gate. "It is God's will," he said. My tongue burned to remind him that women are forbidden to teach, but I dared not.

If you will come here to the Paraclete, master, you too will see and hear Nuntia. May God keep you safe. Farewell.

Letter 13 (ca. 1134)

[To] her beloved husband, father and brother, Abélard, Héloïse, in utmost love and joy:

Each day, evening, and night seems to bring yet more extraordinary manifestations and lessons. Yet I doubt my heart could be lifted into higher exultation than that which Nuntia brought us last night. It being the dark of the moon and we sisters naturally begun our monthly purgations, we therefore hesitated to show ourselves outside the gate when Nuntia bade us go again to the side of the river. The sisters all looked to me, of course, to explain how it was (if it were possible he did not know, with the smell so strong among us) that we felt a lack of propriety in showing ourselves publicly. And so I did remind him of this circumstance and asked that he excuse our attendance on him outside. To our great surprise, this evoked a new lesson from him, on the particular nature of women's bodies.

"It is wrong to hide yourselves in shame, for menstruation is a great glory of nature, which allows humans alone of all animals to separate the functions of sexual generation from those of pleasure, and gives to men and women the power of will over both."

This shocked us, as you may well imagine, and on several counts. "But it says in Genesis," I exclaimed, "that the pain and shame of menstruation is a curse that came down to us through Eve, for tempting Adam to sin." For though many women doubt this precept, it seemed the appropriate response to be made to a man or rather messenger of God.

And so then Nuntia repeated (as he often does when we cite doctrine in objection to his teachings) that Christ had nullified Old-Testament law and that God meant us to use our reason to lift us above lives of repetition and rote such as that which lower animals live. He went on at some length on this subject, amplifying the wonders of the female body, even denying that it was weaker than man's, for how, he said, could woman bear menstruation every month and the great work of pregnancy, labor, and delivery, if she were truly weak? I have become so bold, beloved, that I spoke right out to say that everyone knew that when saying that a woman's body was weak it was in reference to her spiritual and moral, not physical, character. But Nuntia countered me again, asking, if woman were spiritually and morally weak, would God have allotted her such an important task as that of bringing children into the world? Would he not, instead, have chosen men, as being more fit morally and spiritually?

And so saying, Nuntia told us that he would await us at our place on the river and vanished, leaving us to ourselves. At which we broke into such lively discussion that we nearly forgot to go out through the gate to meet him.

Your letter, which my man brought me on his return here yesterday, saddens me, beloved. Now that the texts have begun to be translated more fully, you say you see their stinking taint of heresy (a dismissal that comes strangely from the pen of one who has shown through his own work the manifold differences of doctrinal interpretation among the Fathers).[13] Nuntia has told us that the early Doctors of the Church ruled heretical every text and revelation that threatened their own personal ambitions and control of the Church. They concealed from all future generations the knowledge that Mary Magdalene was among the first apostles (though I wonder that they let stand in the Gospels the fact that she was the first person to see Christ after his death). The early Doctors appropriated vast powers to themselves and tampered with the letters of Saint Paul. And they ignored the most important teachings of their holy master when they emphasized Old-Testament doctrine as it suited their requirements. The copies of the notes I have so far sent you are an explication of how Ecclesia came to be such an overly-dominating mother determined to keep her children in infancy for the whole of their lives. If anyone knows, most beloved, how the power of declaring this one a heretic and that piece of work heresy is abused, it is you. You have yourself been condemned as the author of heresy, as happened at Soissons not long ago. How can you speak so righteously, then, of branding ancient writings, so much closer to the pure teachings of the Christ, heresy?

[13] Héloïse is here referring to one of Abélard's earlier works, *Sic et Non*, a compendium of the diverse positions taken by the most revered theologians in the Church, which while making obvious their continual conflicts of opinion, offered no solution for smoothing them over.

But if you do so because you fear being condemned another time, with
surely a harsher punishment to follow, I
cannot blame you.[14] To be deprived
again of teaching would be more, I
know, than you could bear. For that reason, I assure you now, beforehand, that
I fully absolve you of any and all blame
if you should decide to hand my letters
and notes over to the pope's legate or any
episcopal authority. Doing so, beloved,

[14] Abélard,
condemned by the
Council of Soissons
before a papal legate in
1121, was sentenced
to confinement at the prison
monastery of St. Médard, and
was forced to burn his
theological work on the Trinity.
Through the intervention of
powerful friends, his
confinement was brief.

you would make plain our estrangement and separation and
thereby incur no blame on my account. I will even return your
letters, if it is your will, to be given over with mine so that all
may see that you did the utmost to influence me otherwise.

For all I have been entirely taken up with listening to
Nuntia's lessons and writing and speaking them for others, I
have only in the last few days begun to realize what must
have been the true reason for your insisting that I take the
veil. I knew it could not be only because you had decided to
take monastic vows yourself and feared opposition from the
Church if your wife did not profess them as well, since there
was no question of the Church holding you capable of rendering the debt to me, though I often hoped it was because
you meant to keep us as close as previously, though your mis-
trust in me, making me precede you into orders, told my intellect that that was not so, however much I told myself the
pain and shame of your mutilation made you only seem so
indifferent to me.

Lately, we sisters have begun to talk among ourselves as
we never did before. (No, dearest, I do not believe such talking to be frivolous gossip, which is what you have always said
when urging me to forbid it.) Only now can I tell you, that if
the sisters at Argenteuil had not been so affectionate and tac-
itly sympathetic to me, I would surely have died from your

years of silence and neglect. Of the sisters there, I always shared an especial affinity with Marie, and so it has been mainly with her that I have lately held private conversation (such as you would never grant me). Sister Marie comes, like you, from Brittany, and has spent much less of her life clois-tered than I, who apart from those two-and-a-half scant years living with my uncle and then briefly at Le Pallet in your family's chateau, can remember no other life, since I was brought to Argenteuil when I was at most four years of age. A few days ago I mentioned to her briefly that I had become a nun only because it had been your will that I do so. She nodded and remarked, "To protect his honor." Though I have long known you provided my dowry to maintain your honor, I confess I did not know exactly what she meant by saying you had likely urged me to take holy orders for that reason, and said so. And then she said that among well-born laity, nothing is so important to a man than that his wife or sister or mother be above suspicion of unchasteness, and that a man such as you, of a knight's family, though he had renounced the life of a warrior and the patrimony of an eldest son, would worry about his reputation were any woman attached to him not either cloistered or kept closely under lock and key.

I remind you, beloved, if this is true, that you have sev-ered your bond with me, just as surely as if the Church had dissolved our marriage. My love for you remains as deep as it has ever been, though I see now that of us both only I ever took the perfection of it as the goal toward which to strive. I could wish for nothing better than for you to come here, to learn at the feet of Nuntia, as I am doing. You are disturbed that he tells me the politics and dealings of the most impor-tant men of France, Brittany, Burgundy, and Champagne with the pope. But I tell you again: you have no obligation to en-danger yourself for my sake. As for myself, I know my task and duty and will not fear to perform it. Nuntia warns me that if the Church and nobility continue in their ways, there will in future generations (not yours, or mine, or Astrolabe's, but in time yet to come) be an ever increasing slaughter of innocents in the name of God, sanctioned and even demanded by the Church. There will be more crusades, and vast massacres of heretics, and then the deaths of tens of thousands of women on the spurious grounds that they consort with Satan, and then Inquisitions against Jews, Saracens, and Christians out of favor with the Church, followed by even greater religious wars among Christian factions killing tens of thousands and spreading ever more fear and hatred, including the spread of this pestilence of violence to lands in distant parts of the earth, by which warriors and disease carried by priests sent to convert their inhabitants will kill millions and vilely enslave even more. What is my life in the balance against so unimaginably many lives in the future, most beloved? Where you had left me only the life of hypocritical piety to lead, now I may savor the quiet joy of doing God's work. I am indeed blessed, beloved, and I thank God for having chosen me.

As this may be the last letter of mine you choose to read, I bid you farewell with special tenderness and beg that you pray for me in my hour of danger, as we here always prayed for you when the wicked monks of your abbey imperiled your very existence.

Letter 14 (ca. 1135)

[To] her most beloved one, Abélard, Héloïse, in the love of the Light:

Though we have the greatest need for conducting our communications with discretion, given the nature of your mission I believe you bear an even greater need for the constant reminder of our love and our faith that you will succeed. Jean, the man who carries this to you, has my full trust. His wife conceived, she said, only after having been touched by the Light that is in me, thus moving him to the fullest expression of gratitude. This letter, he has most solemnly vowed, will be placed into no other hands than your own. Though we have only a very general notion of your itinerary, Jean will travel until he finds you.

Since your departure I have thought often and at length about how the Light has inspired a change in your heart with as intensive a searching and sifting of detail as I once applied to the memories of our love and your abandonment of me. Perhaps in your absence I need to reassure myself continually that I have not imagined the last months, that your willingness to take instruction from Nuntia and to study and discuss Nuntia's teachings with me and my sisters were not merely the phantasms of a yearning, wishful mind.

Beloved, when you came to us last summer, possessed of the fiercest determination to remove us from the Paraclete and cleanse the oratory of what you assumed must be great supernatural evil, I despaired that even the Light could touch your harsh, obdurate heart. Human beings, Nuntia frequently reminds us, seldom perceive what truly troubles them, and avoid acknowledging or even seeing what causes them deep pain, fear, or shame. Which is why I have begun to form the idea that perhaps for all these years if you avoided meeting me, or when meeting me even looking into my face, it was because the very sight of me caused you pain by confronting you with a truth you would rather forget.

My heart almost stopped when I saw you ride into the encampment outside the gate where I was prophesying and preaching, for you looked so very exhausted and ill, and I could see that the old injury in your shoulder was paining you, such that both fear and compassion surged through me. But then the harshness of your words and manner to me, beyond all of my experience of you, shocked me so that I forgot your wretched state and wanted only to remove the force of your anger from the people to whom I had been preaching love. But when, having passed inside the gate, you told me you could see no other help for it than to take me to Le Pallet, to confine me there, if I did not return directly to my senses, I could feel only pity for the helplessness and frustration your anger only thinly veiled. What woman or man would not wish to comfort a beloved so distressed as you were? Yet you would not be comforted, and I knew would not listen to anything I or my sisters might say to you. And so while you were occupied instructing our portress Sister Bertrande on letting no one pass either in or out the gate without your explicit permission, I murmured the prayer Nuntia had given me to call him at my need.

You first strode to the oratory, your greatest concern, fearful that we had somehow contaminated or damaged it. There you were confronted by the Light, which you had somehow forgotten, and you knew, standing in its presence, that it was not in any way evil. Still, though under its most powerful radiance, after you kneeling thanked God for having kept you safe during your journey, you asked his assistance in "cleansing" the oratory and "restoring to goodness and sanity" the sisters to whom you had entrusted it. Much subdued, but still determined to "cleanse" the Paraclete of either madness or evil (which one you did not know), you ordered me to go into Chapter, where you would address all the sisters, and then went yourself to the library, to summon whichever sisters were then laboring at their desks.

I did not see what happened when you saw the brother from Cluny, bent over the Light-given texts on my desk. But surely the sight must have shaken your conviction? Several minutes later, when we were assembled in Chapter, and after we had each knelt and kissed your ring, you stood before us, your face wretchedly tired and grim, your eyes, quenched by a desolation even your previous sorrows had never evinced, always and assiduously avoiding the very sight of me. There we sat quietly around you, on the benches lining the walls, our hands in our laps, our hearts open to you, our founder, and to your obvious distress. And I wondered that you could not feel our warmth and compassion enfolding you, who were standing so straight and rigid before us, refusing all offers of refreshment, declining even to seat yourself though trembling with the exhaustion of the long ride behind you. In silence your eyes moved from face to face, looking at each of my sisters in turn (though never at me). And then you sighed, so heavily, as heavily as you did after the first time you lay with me, no, more heavily, as heavily as you did that first time you left me at Le Pallet, pregnant with our son, knowing that only by my remaining there could both you and I be safe from my uncle's wrath, though we neither of us thought we could stand to be so long parted. Forgive me, beloved, I know you do not wish me to recall times past. But when I reach for comparisons by which to relate a particular experience, it is our past history that always springs to mind, lending me the images by which to measure and judge our words, thoughts, and deeds, words I can expect you to understand.

"My daughters, for whom I feel the most especial care," you began wearily, as if the weight of obligation you felt pressing your spirit was nearly more than you could bear. In these first words, what I had suspected from your determined avoidance of the very sight of me was confirmed. Never have you addressed me as "daughter," and thus I knew that you meant to exclude me from your speech, since you otherwise would have said "sister and daughters," as you usually do when you address us collectively. "It is a sad and fearful thing when the shepherd, falling prey to vicious illness, leads his flock astray, into danger," you said. "Though the sheep may suspect they are being led wrongly and may wonder at aberrations they sense in their master, yet they know it is not their place to question or defy, whether singly or collectively, his commands. This, I am grieved to say, is what has happened here. But fear not, I have come to restore order, and so to lead this flock back to solid, safe ground. And though you will feel great compassion for your shepherd, you will do so from safety, whence you can assist her through your most favored prayers to God for her swift recovery."

Did you not think, dearest, there might be something wrong in telling my sisters they were sheep? Did you not see the compassion in their faces for you? Or feel how they were waiting, waiting, waiting either for me to speak, or Nuntia to appear? Sister Marie, sitting close beside me, held herself composed and still, such that only the whiteness of her tightly clasped knuckles betrayed her distress. Later she joked that she had thought to say that she, the infirmarian, had detected no illness in the abbess, but that she, a mere nun, dared not— not to the man whom bishops and other abbots would contest only under the shield of a Church council convoked with the determination to silence him. No, my sisters waited for me to speak, to bring you the truth, for it never occurred to them, all in such awe of my learning, that if I spoke you would do anything but listen attentively.

But Nuntia appeared at that moment, only a few paces before you, in a column of light shining bright in the chamber's dimness. "Peter Abélard of Pallet," he addressed you.[15] "Master of Schools. Abbot of Gildas de Rhuys. Greetings. I am Nuntia, sent by God to bring the Light to the children of the earth."

And you, dearest Pierre, crossed yourself— to ward off danger, a gesture being so foreign to you that it startled me, such that I did not hear your response to Nuntia's greeting.

"You need not fear me," Nuntia said. "Rather, I have come to turn you from the road the Church has taken by mistake, a road leading to a virtual hell on earth, which men, imagining themselves shepherds of their brothers and sisters, whom they liken to sheep, have driven them to take."

I will never forget the grimness of your mouth as you bade Nuntia "Begone!" as though he were a fox poaching, or a demon playing tricks on your eyes.

"Let us reason together, Peter Abélard," Nuntia said next. "Forget your superstitious fears, for they are worthy only of

[15]We have retained "Petrus" in the text in order to distinguish it from Héloïse's use of "Pierre" below.

the heretic hunter, whose prey you have been from the time you began trodding on your own masters' toes."

At which you rubbed and rubbed your hands over your face (not even realizing you did so) and straightened your shoulders, as though you had just recalled who you were and the ground on which you had long been fighting. And you said: "Whatever you are, you have been filling these women's heads with dangerous and arrant nonsense. Telling them to preach. Telling them it is their place to challenge Church authority. Plying them with texts ruled centuries ago to be heresy. Stirring women to rebellion is hardly the exponent of reason."

"I speak only the truth," Nuntia answered you. "It is the truth that women preached in the earliest days of the Church. It is the truth that their menstrual pain has nothing to do with Eve and everything to do with a flexibility of choice given to humans above all other animals. It is the truth that if misogynist beliefs are not soon discredited, they will before long bloom into a terrible scourge against women from which it will take centuries and centuries to recover. You know yourself the tendency in the Church to shed blood in the name of Christ. You, Peter Abélard, have never favored crusades. Nor do you favor the persecution of Jews. Yet if the mass madness of the Church is not prevented from developing, not only women, but diverse peoples throughout the world will perish from its excesses. Of this I have been sent to warn you."

And so it began, Nuntia's explication and warnings, and his discussion with you of the early Doctors, which more than anything else shook your confidence. And though we had soon to break for Vespers, you talked with Nuntia through the night, even until Matins, after which Nuntia said we must all get some sleep.

Nuntia told me (though you did not) that what tipped the balance was his close attention to Christ's teachings, with which you could not argue. You always did have trouble with the issue of St. Peter's passing on the keys to his successors. And though you thought the apostles and early Doctors must have been exceptional, yet you have long known full well what men in high places are like, how they struggle and connive and lie when it suits their personal ambitions. And so, applying reason to what Nuntia told you, you knew that he had to be right.

Yet how difficult it has been for you to permit me even to teach. When Nuntia insisted that you not teach in my stead, you wanted to wrestle with him as Jacob wrestled with the angel. And it offends your sense of decorum, still, to see me and my sisters speaking freely to one another without what you call a good reason for it. There is so much of what Nuntia has shown us that you cannot seem to understand. Dearest, most beloved Pierre, I believe this will come, too.

I wish neither to hurt nor to scold you. But I feel the time is appropriate for telling you of a discussion Nuntia and I had some months past, for I believe you will think carefully about it now, rather than react with instant, unconsidered anger, especially as you have so much time to spend now on horseback, which you have always said provides as excellent opportunity for exercise of one's intellect as for meditation. When Nuntia insisted that I continue to receive special instruction from him even after you first opened your heart to his words, I demanded of him why, and also as to the reason he had not been giving special instruction to my sisters as well, or himself preach to the people assembled outside the gate. And he replied thus: "I speak to you rather than to your sisters or the encampment at large because of your mastery of Latin. Though I am an intelligence that understands the vernacular and many of its dialects, I do not speak it with any facility and thus rely on you to transmit my words to them. And I do not undertake to instruct Peter Abélard as I do you because his heart and intellect are not sufficiently open to hearing my words and understanding them. On the day that he has opened himself to hear all that you say to him, and on that day only, will he be ready to receive the instruction I have been giving you."

Beloved, I could not deny that your heart and intellect are closed to most of what I say, or rather are closed to everything I say that does not echo what you have already said to me. I felt deeply saddened when Nuntia said these words to me. But he told me I must not be, for he said that the hearts of men and women are always open to the change that is love, no matter who they have been and what they have done, though it may seem to everyone who knows them that their hearts are made rather of stone than of flesh and blood. And I laughed a little at that, for no one who knows you truly would say that your heart is made of stone, even now after all that has been done to destroy you.

As you know, Nuntia says that love of God is not hatred of others, beloved, but that it is the deepest love of all, the deepest, most far-flung love of self and others together, in community. The seed of that love has always been in you. And whatever you say now, it began to sprout in our love, and would have grown green and luscious if my uncle had not done his best to kill it. May it with good tending and care spring to life now, and flourish in the heat and glory of the Light!

Our prayers and thoughts are with you as you pursue the difficult mission of winning support for us from our friends of old. Remember, the Light burns brightly here, without ceasing.

Letter 15 (ca. 1135)

[To] her most beloved one, Abélard, Héloïse, in the love of the Light:

We were all exceedingly pleased to receive, through Jean, your letter, both because it assured us of your safety and well-being, and because, too, it brought us the welcome news that the Abbot of St. Denis has promised us his protection and will be shortly writing us a letter to that effect. We are pleased, also (though less surprised) that the Bishop of Chartres has pledged us support. If it were not that the Abbot of Clairveaux had just been here, I, like you, would have wondered if even Suger's "protection" would amount to much, given his early opposition to any of the French clergy's attending the council in Pisa in May— until Bernard's will prevailed in this matter, too.

Yes, that is one of my several pieces of news. Bernard has indeed been here and gone. You can imagine how my heart fluttered with misgiving when the news was brought to me that the Abbot of Clairveaux himself was at the gate, requesting a night's hospitality as well as a word with me. And let me say first, that my last important visitor, our Count himself, had only two weeks previous left us uneasy, for though he agreed to give us land nearer Troyes for establishing a daughter house (which he very well knew we needed, because of the many new novitiates we have lately attracted), he said he was very disturbed at what he had been hearing in the villages as well as in Troyes and Meaux as to our teachings here. I looked very straightly at him and tried to hold his eyes to mine, and said that we were teaching only what the angel Nuntia had been speaking to me. I believe, beloved, that the aura around my head, and the Light in the oratory, combined to quell his protest, for he quickly offered me the land and promised to send a deed of it in writing. And yet he may regret it later, when he is away from here, and his disquiet over the ferment we have inspired in his domain returns in force. I see trouble from him in the future, however excellent the benefits he has bestowed on you in the past. He made several remarks about how unsafe it was for a group of women to be surrounded by so many hundreds of uncouth serfs and townsfolk. He expressed anger that serfs from all over Champagne had been leaving their villages to join our encampment and reminded me that the Paraclete's own provisioning depended heavily upon these same serfs' labor, which was owed rightfully to him, their lord. I have discussed this with Nuntia, beloved, and he believes it will be important for us to win support among at least some of the laity. The manorial system is doomed, he told me, though most of the lords will fight tooth and nail to preserve it, since they (and we cloistered religious) benefit most from it.

But to return to the Abbot of Clairveaux. When I heard that he was at the gate, I went out myself, for respect, to meet him. And so he first beheld me in full sunlight and did not see the aura. When I knelt to kiss his ring, he called me sister (as the Abbot of Cluny had done) and remarked jokingly that though whatever was going on here at the Paraclete had removed his rival, Master Peter, from the Schools, thus allowing him a free hand at winning his young men to conversion, yet it seemed that I had become a new rival, draining the countryside of all other preachers' converts. And then, as I rose to my feet, he said, "What is this I hear, that women are preaching and prophesying? Do you not know, with all your great learning, that such things should be left to men?" That he did not expect me to answer he made clear by introducing me, before I could speak, to the monk accompanying him.

And so I led him and his companion to the oratory, to see the Light bathing the altar. But while we were walking, at a point just after we had entered the main building, I heard him suddenly gasp. I moved my head a little, perhaps to see what had disturbed him, and saw from the corner of my eye that he had halted a pace or two behind me. And when I turned to face him, he fell to his knees, and whispered "Lady!"[16] And his companion did fall to his knees likewise. You can imagine my surprise, beloved, considering Bernard's usual suspicions regarding women. But perhaps you will be less surprised, since you know so well how drawn the abbot is to special manifestations of Grace.

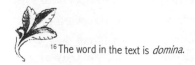

[16] The word in the text is *domina*.

"It is not to me you should kneel, Father," I said to him. "I but carry a bit of the Light in my person, by comparison with the Light in the oratory. And the Light itself is not there to be worshiped, but to help open our hearts to love and our eyes to truth."

The abbot looked startled. "Then God has made you a fount of grace, lady. From which we his children would be privileged to drink."

The metaphor troubled me as soon as I heard it (and continues to trouble me the more it is repeated). I wanted to protest, yet hesitated to speak too quickly, lest I say something I might later wish the power to take back. Fortunately, he and his companion rose to their feet and continued with me to the oratory.

I do not think I need go into further detail describing the abbot's conversion (to borrow his own favorite word) to the Light. The library, as you might expect, did not much interest him, though he observed the scroll on my desk with respect. It did not seem necessary to call Nuntia to appear to him, since he saw no evil in any of the Light's manifestations and apologized profusely for having criticized me for presuming to preach. If he knew what Nuntia says about the Light and intelligence, would it not, I wonder, have gone differently with him? For surely Nuntia's teaching and the Light pose a challenge to the abbot's clinging to the "enigma" of faith. When the abbot left the next day, Nuntia said that it was well— and added that we can be assured now that we have averted the disaster of your being tried for heresy after the king's and the antipope's deaths. Bernard may obstruct our message by misconstruing it, says Nuntia, but will not oppose it. Surely, if that is true, your mission must succeed. With both Bernard and Suger on our side, how can we lose?

My last piece of news is this: Nuntia has given Sister Marthe instruction on the means of constructing a machine for copying texts in great number, rather than one at a time. One of the scrolls on my desk provided images of several different machines that would do this. Sister Marthe is very clever; you may recall that it is she who devised the system for carrying water from the Ardusson through pipes to the kitchens and latrines, and who has plans for setting up a mill for making paper. The very simplest (though not what Nuntia calls the "optimal") machine requires the carving of letters or words on wood blocks, which, inked, will reproduce again and again the same piece of text for as many times as one wishes. Marthe has set a great number of people to making the blocks and carving them. Nuntia considers this is of the utmost importance, for he says that everyone who is capable must be taught to read and write and be given access to texts (which would of course be impossible without there being many copies of books available for people to read).

You say that nothing in my letter hurt or angered you. If that is true, I am glad. And yet it may be that you simply allow nothing past the high stone walls you have erected around your heart, neither love nor pain nor fear nor pleasure of any sort. Love is not an arid thought of the mind, beloved, but a living diffusion of heat that can both warm and scorch, heal and hurt. Do not flee it, Pierre, I entreat you. You think I do not know your suffering, that I neither recognize nor understand your pain. Yet only consider, beloved, that in your way you have inflicted upon me almost the exact punishment my uncle inflicted on you— the only difference being that one sort of pleasure is still open to me which is closed to you, and that it is always possible that I could— if I chose to defy you, and embrace the world— again be a woman in the way in which you cannot be a man (though it is unlikely I would ever care to do so). If you have had your manhood taken from you, you yourself have taken my womanhood. You once feared ridicule and shame for your mutilation, but only the lowest of your enemies ever thinks you less of a master for your loss of member. And do you believe I have escaped ridicule? I, the subject of all those famed songs, locked up for all of my youth out of the sight of the world?

But as when I was known as your whore, I have not allowed it to signify to me. To say that I neither recognize nor understand your pain is too simple a dismissal of my argument, beloved. And so I pray that the Light will open your heart and make you whole, as perhaps you have never before been.

Letter 16 (ca. 1135)

[To] her beloved Peter Abélard, Héloïse:

I am relieved to hear that after you leave Bourges, Cluny will be your next and penultimate destination. I beg of you, dearest, rest there a while before you begin your return here. It would give the abbot the greatest pleasure to have your learning within his walls and also allow your back to heal a little. I know how impatiently you travel, and have little doubt that you have driven your body to the limits of what it can endure. It has always been your way to disregard your physical needs to the extent that your body can stand it.

Nuntia has been telling me that I must think of setting aside time to be spent undisturbed by duties of any sort, in which to bend my entire self to contemplation and reflection of all that he and I have been speaking since he first appeared to me. Last week he began discussing some of the texts with me. And yesterday morning after Lauds he told me that the last text was being copied now, that when it is finished there will be no more "displayed" (as he says) at my desk. He said also that the last text is the most important for me to study. And he urged that I translate it at once, so that I may read it with him anon. I thought that because Nuntia said it was so important it would be best to have both Brother Étienne and myself translate it independently. Brother Étienne, therefore, has already begun work on the pages that Denise has so far copied out. Just before dinner today he came to me, as I was about to enter the refectory, and whispered to me that the name Heloissa occurs often in the text. Something Nuntia said (a cryptic remark about the text containing a prophesy) makes me wonder if the name might actually refer to <u>me</u>. The text, by the way, is entitled "The Book of Mary, Sister of Martha and Lazarus."

Something else, most strange, has occurred that causes me not a little unease. The Light in the oratory, it seems to me (and to my sisters and everyone else as well), has acquired a golden tint. I do not know quite when it changed, for I believe it may have happened gradually, since the difference became apparent not because of its suddenly being different than it had been a few hours before, but because I noticed that it made our skin look warm and almost tawny rather than ghostly pale as it had done originally. When Nuntia next appeared, my mind was on the difference, and so I examined him, too, and discovered that his appearance had changed as well. He appears even more elongated, yet rounder, almost womanly now. And the pinkish tinge of his tunic has deepened to rose, while his headgear has acquired jeweled studs.

When I asked Nuntia about these differences, he stood completely motionless, his face a virtual mask for at least as long as it would take to say the Our Father. And I began to think, in fright, of the idols in the Old Testament, the graven images that neither hear nor speak. But then his face became lifelike again and full of movement, and his eyes looked into mine. "Already significant change has begun to take effect," he said to me. "These differences you note are a sign of that, and are caused by what we call 'phase shifts.' Which means the time set for me to spend here is nearly fulfilled. Soon the 'differential' will be too great for me to be assured of continuity. And I must leave you before that happens. We have little time left for instruction, Heloissa Beatissima. We must spend the time remaining well."

Nuntia has lately taught me to think differently about the creation of Adam and Eve. The creation of Eve from Adam's rib symbolizes, Nuntia says, the splitting of the human soul and mind into two parts, Life and Spirit, wherein the characteristics of embodiment are put all onto Eve, the woman, whereby all sin is blamed on her (and thus on embodiment). But God, Nuntia says, requires that each of us become whole— such that Spirit reclaims Life and Life reclaims Spirit. For Eve is the luminous Epinoia, which is to say Life. In taking Epinoia from Adam, man was cast into the shadow of death, and, becoming only Spirit, sank into the ignorance of darkness and the desire for Life, from which he had been separated. And this is the significance of the marriage metaphor, namely that within each soul Life must be joined with Spirit, and not be denied simply because Spirit so greatly desires (and has therefore learned to hate) that from which it has been parted. It is Epinoia, Nuntia says, who brings Light to the darkness of Spirit. It is she who is the mother of the living, who was first called Sophia, which as you know is Greek for wisdom.

I do not believe, my heart,[17] that Nuntia means us to understand the texts he has sent us as an admonition to forsake all physical things and earthly relations. I have asked him about our (former) love (in a general way, without citing our own particular case), and he responded that physical love is not wrong unless it involves a lack of respect, one partner to the other. He made scathing remarks about the abusive treatment so many priests and prelates afford to the women who live with them as their concubines; but said that marriages blessed by the Church were seldom any better, for only rarely do men and women intimately related treat one another with true respect. As for monastic vows of chastity, he said that the original idea had been a good one and had much favored women in the early days of Christianity, for it had freed them from bonds that had been most oppressive to them and had interfered with their spiritual commitment to the Christ. But he said that chastity was not essential for leading a strongly moral and spiritual life, and though it could be helpful to the

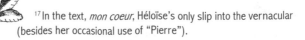

[17] In the text, *mon coeur*, Héloïse's only slip into the vernacular (besides her occasional use of "Pierre").

individual, it could also become too important, such that it prevents spiritual growth by developing into a personal demon that is always there to be wrestled.

And finally, I will add one last thing that he said, because it is something you once knew and of which I have long felt you needed reminding. Origen is no fit exemplar on which to model yourself. The accident of your mutilation makes him attractive to you, and perhaps once was helpful for bringing you to regard yourself as still worthy to both serve God and teach. But since you now know that, you have no need of a model, and would do well to shed such a deformed view of spiritual life. Nuntia says, beloved, that your own spiritual growth depends upon it.

When I have learned what is in this last text, I will write straightaway to you. Since I expect you to be found for some time at Cluny, I will feel free to send you a letter at once even if Jean should not have returned from carrying you this one. May the Light infuse your heart and spirit with love, my most beloved. We pray for you daily.

Letter 17 (ca 1135)

[To] her beloved Peter Abélard, Héloïse:

What I have to tell you in this letter is of the utmost importance, my heart.[18] I would have wished to consult with you first (although I do not believe doing so would have changed anything, it would surely have been a comfort to me if I had been able), but because Nuntia will be leaving us shortly, probably before your return, it was not possible.

Let me begin by telling you about "The Book of Mary, Sister of Martha and Lazarus." Its first sentences read: "This is the testimony of Mary, the sister of Martha and Lazarus.

[18] Again, the vernacular *mon coeur* is used.

And it came to pass several years after the death of Jesus, born of woman in order to be the Christ, that the Domination Nuntia appeared to Mary. 'Behold,' he said to her. 'You, Mary, have seen how the disciples of Jesus have ignored his teachings and made a mockery of his redemption of humankind. You have heard how they have denied the truth of the Resurrection spoken by Mary Magdalene, whom he favored above them. God and his mother, Sophia, and all the entities in the heavens grieve, because it appears that the Word was brought to the world only to be misspoken and squandered.'"

The text then gives another version of Jesus's life, similar to those in the Gospels, but with certain differences that (except for the description of Jesus's appearances after the Resurrection) are more a matter of emphasis than substance. It then condemns Peter's pride and ambition, and his lack of comprehension of Jesus's teaching, and prophesies the creation of the Church as we know it (though describing it as a "scourge" rather than as a mother to its children). But the prophesy does not end there. The last half of the text has to do with our times— with "the year of our Lord Eleven Hundred Thirty-four when Nuntia will appear before the Abbess Héloïse at the monastery of the Paraclete," and "the year of our Lord Eleven Hundred Thirty-five when the Abbess Héloïse will conceive, without intercourse, the second Christ, Magdalene." Yes, beloved, it says that exactly. You can imagine my shock when Brother Étienne (who began working on his translation of the text before I started mine) told me.

This text prophesies that Nuntia will appear before me and fill me with Light. And it says that in June of 1135, at the time of the full moon, a great pool of Light will descend upon me and will cause me to conceive. And that immediately after I conceive Nuntia and the Light will withdraw, having fulfilled their purpose. And that in the spring of the next year I will be delivered of a daughter, Magdalene, who will be a second Christ to the world. But that this time, the world will be more open and prepared to hear the Christ's message and to learn from the Christ's teaching.

It will be our task, my heart, to teach Magdalene and rear her to her task, and to keep her safe from the forces that will seek to destroy her as the first Christ was destroyed.

After expounding the text to me, Nuntia asked if I consented to bear Magdalene, which surprised me greatly. And when he saw my surprise, he said that no woman should be asked to bear a child without first giving consent! And he asked if I believed that Mary, the mother of Jesus, had not consented. And then, still seeing my confusion and disbelief, said that he had discussed with Marthe the ways there are for women to prevent conception. So I said to Nuntia that I would like to speak with you first, being my husband. And then he told me that there was no time for that. Which recalled to me the prophesy, since this is June and the full moon was almost at that time upon us.

And indeed, beloved, last night the moon was full. And last night, in Chapter, surrounded by all my sisters and in the presence of Nuntia, Father Louis, Brother Étienne, the Abbot of Clairveaux, and the Bishop of Troyes (whom I specially called to us, at Nuntia's urgent instruction), as the text prophesied, a pool of Light descended upon me. Following Nuntia's instructions, I had beforehand fasted for three days, remaining the entire time in my cell, in solitude, praying and meditating on the Book of Mary. And when the moon was well in the sky, we filed into Chapter, and there I knelt in the center of the room, as my sisters chanted a Gloria. My eyes were closed as I silently spoke the prayer Nuntia had taught me, and the Light showered down upon me. And though outwardly I could hear my sisters chanting, I heard Nuntia, as though speaking directly into my ear (as he has often spoken to me), intoning words in a very deep, throbbing voice. What he said I cannot now remember, for it happened as in a dream. When the chanting ceased and I had risen to my feet, I found myself singing the Magnificat (without having had any thought or intention for doing so). And my joy and happiness was supreme, as I have never before felt it, as the Light flooded and almost blinded me with its rich golden brilliance. And when I finished, Nuntia held his arms high over his head, and a torch appeared above his helmet, and he exclaimed, "Ave, Heloissa Beatissima, et Vale!" And then both he and the Light vanished.

At the bishop's urging, we went then to the oratory, to make a special mass. We found the Light had gone from there, too, and were deeply saddened. They say there is still an aura around my head; but I have grown so used to being able to talk to Nuntia whenever I wish that I am desolated by his departure. I am to rely on my own heart and intellect, he told me. But whatever he has taught us about growing into adults from our spiritual infancy, I feel like a babe abandoned by its nurse.

I cannot say for certain whether I am indeed with child.[19] In my heart I believe it, though my intellect tells me it is not possible to conceive without coitus. We will know soon enough. And in the meantime, I wish you will speed here to us with all the haste that is safe. I would have you love Magdalene and nurture her according to Nuntia's instruction. If there is new life in me, beloved, it is a miracle. And miracles are given that our hearts be opened to love and our minds to truth.

[19] As a matter of historical record, Héloïse bore a daughter named Magdalene in March of the year 1136. Though an immaculate conception was declared, and Bernard of Cîteaux claimed to have witnessed it, later scholars have speculated that Héloïse conceived by a secret lover, a fact it would have been a scandal for her to disclose. Magdalene, of course, was the focal personality at the center of the Magdalenian Reform, which Héloïse initiated. It has long been a matter of debate whether the Magdalenian Reform (which included, of course, such major changes as the admission of women to the priesthood, universal literacy as a Church priority, and the gradual democratization and decentralization of Church governance) influenced the transformation of the manorial system into communally-owned and managed cooperatives, or vice versa. Obviously these documents, if released, would impinge on the debate considerably.

About the Author

From childhood through adolescence and into her early adult years, **L. Timmel Duchamp** devoted herself mind, body, and soul to writing and performing music. Though trauma briefly derailed her creative drive onto an academic track, she soon found herself, at a whim, writing a scandalously shameless *roman à clef* for the amusement of her friends and colleagues. Seduced by this brief taste of the fierce and delirious pleasures of fiction-writing, she deserted the academy and abandoned herself to writing many more novels. Six years later, in 1986, she wrote her first short story, "Welcome, Kid, to the Real World." This story, which made the 1996 Tiptree Award's short list, did not see print for ten years. Duchamp wrote three more novels and several more short stories before she made her first sale in 1989, to Susanna Sturgis (*Memories and Visions: Women's Fantasy and Science Fiction*, Vol. 1) for "O's Story." Since then she has made more than two dozen magazine and anthology sales, of which one has been a Sturgeon Award finalist, another a Nebula finalist, and three shortlisted for the Tiptree Award; several of her stories have been nominated for the Hugo.

Duchamp considers her years of music composition to be a continuing significant influence on her work. Like many composers in the late '60s and early '70s, with each new composition she devised new forms of notation and invented new musical structures with the understanding that form, content, and style are inseparable. Her engagement with prose forms might not appear to the casual eye to be as radical as her past engagement with musical forms, but she views the narrative process as similarly contingent on the inseparability of form, content, and style. Her thoughts about narrative, a complete bibliography of her work, and a few more of her stories can be found on her website:
http://ltimmel.home.mindspring.com.

About the Type

This book was set in a digital version of Monotype Walbaum, available through AGFA-Monotype. The original typeface was designed by Justus Erich Walbaum who came to typography via the unusual route of confectionery. He taught himself engraving while making his own pudding moulds working in a pastry shop. At night, he started engraving music types. Eventually he set up his own foundry in a town called Goslar.

In 1802, just before his town was to be incorporated into Prussia, he left for Weimar where he established another successful foundry. His classical types were quite popular until the fashion changed, after which his name disappeared until the 1920s, when it was revived as Monotype Walbaum.

Forthcoming from Aqueduct Press

Coming Fall 2004, a new novel by Gwyneth Jones, 1991 winner of the James Tiptree award for her book *White Queen*. This new novel, *Life*, is a richly textured science fiction biography of a near-future biologist, the brilliant Anna Senoz, who makes a momentous (though initially disbelieved) discovery about the X and Y chromosomes. *Life* explores the workings of gender not only in its protagonist's life but in the practice of science and in the academic scientific community as well. And it asks sophisticated questions about the future of feminism that need very badly, these days, to be articulated.

Coming Spring 2005, *Alanya to Alanya* by L. Timmel Duchamp. This gripping political thriller is the first book of The Marq'ssan Cycle, which Aqueduct Press will publish in five volumes.

Coming Fall 2005, *The Same River Twice*, an anthology of short fiction about change.

What reviewers say about L. Timmel Duchamp's fiction:

For several years now, L. Timmel Duchamp has been writing the kind of quiet, under-the-skin science fiction stories that resonate in the reader's mind long after the stories end."
—*Inscriptions*

Duchamp's confidence, coupled with her precision, gives her fiction the same authority as her literary criticism. And like her criticism, her stories are complex and layered, requiring the reader to pay attention and think about what she says. Each sentence is carefully crafted, and the overall structure seems thoroughly planned. . . .

I discovered Duchamp's work through her essays—her article on Mary Gentle's *The Architecture of Desire in Lady Churchill's Rosebud Wristlet* No. 8 impressed me greatly because of her complex feminist analysis—and then sought out her fiction. I have now reached the point that I will go out of my way to buy any book or magazine with one of her stories in it. (I'm begging for an anthology here; I hope some publisher is reading this.)
—Nancy Jane Moore, "SF by Starlight"

L. Timmel Duchamp is always interesting, always provocative, one of the most exciting writers to emerge in the past decade.
—Rich Horton, *Tangent Online*

Duchamp unwinds a series of sharp observations about the subjectivity of historical truth. . . biting satire on the various academic theories about Medieval History. . .an indictment against all objectivity, especially concerning relationships between men and women.
—*Tangent*